REVOLUTION STREET

REVOLUTION STREET

AMIR HASSAN CHEHELTAN

Translated by Paul Sprachman

A Oneworld book

First published in North America, Great Britain and Australia by
Oneworld Publications, 2014
First published in German by Kirchheim, 2009

Hardback ISBN 978-1-85168-984-2
ebook ISBN 978-1-78074-224-3

Printed and bound by CPI Group (UK) Ltd, Croydon, CR0 4YY

Oneworld Publications
10 Bloomsbury Street
London WC1B 3SR
England

REVOLUTION STREET

1

Fattah raised his head and looked over at the young nurse with tired, heavy-lidded eyes. Something was bothering him. He held up his gloved hands. The nurse returned his look, her eyebrows raised questioningly. Fattah barked, 'Open it!'

Still confused, the nurse looked nervously back at Fattah, but had no idea what he wanted her to do. 'Unbutton my collar!' Fattah croaked. 'I'm choking!' And to get her to understand the urgency of his predicament, he made his eyes bulge and gasped for breath.

A pale young woman, her eyes closed, lay on a hospital bed covered with a grimy yellow sheet, spotted with blue and purple stains faded from repeated washing. Her bare, skinny legs were bent at the knees, splayed open under the glaring bright light of a lamp hanging from the ceiling by a chain. She was trembling slightly, as if feverish, and moaning softly through slightly parted lips.

A dull, murky light filtered through the narrow basement windows. The panes were spattered with mud and partly obscured by thick dust and mounds of trash piled up outside. There were no curtains, which was a considerable risk.

Outside, a motorcycle suddenly roared past, and the girl on the bed snapped open her eyes and groaned. The doctor and nurse looked up abruptly.

The nurse peeled off her gloves, one after the other, and undid the doctor's top button. Fattah took a quick breath and said, 'Finally . . . Now the next one; open the next one too!'

Breathing in deeply, keeping his half-open eyes on her, he said, 'Thank you.' and let out a huge sigh, which smacked the nurse in the face with the sour smell of fermented dough and rotten meat. He closed his eyes in obvious satisfaction.

The girl on the narrow bed slowly turned her head and looked at them out of the corner of her eye. Then she bit her lip and let out another moan. She was clearly in pain.

Fattah's flushed, flabby double chin had settled back into his loosened collar. He glanced down at the girl and grumbled, 'These whores! They give it away for free, but when it comes time to get married, all of a sudden they remember they're virgins only from the neck up!'

There was something malicious in his tone of voice, and he looked around as if to see the effect on his patient and the nurse.

'Sluts!' the nurse agreed.

Fattah resumed his work. He took a piece of sterile gauze from a stainless-steel tray and cleaned the area between the girl's legs. 'Hurts, doesn't it?' he said with pleasure in his voice.

The girl's eyes flickered open and she nodded. Fattah said drily, 'You're not at a party, my dear. This is a surgery! You should've thought of that before!'

Then, indicating the stainless-steel tray, he said to the nurse, 'Pass me that.'

The nurse pushed the cart closer to him. Fattah picked up a pair of scissors. When the girl saw the scissors, she began to wince and whimper again. Fattah scowled at her and, with hate in his voice, said, 'Quiet! I don't want to hear another peep out of you, understand?'

Without changing his expression, he stared at her for a few moments. The girl looked at him now in terror and pleaded with her eyes, but Fattah continued to glare at her. The girl winced again. Small beads of sweat, which had formed on her temples, now came together, moistening the fine hairs along her face.

Fattah bent his head and pried the girl's thighs open. Then he brought his head closer and held his hand out, saying to the nurse, 'Flashlight!'

The nurse switched on the flashlight and held it out. Fattah had her point it between the girl's legs and said, 'Look! The tramp!'

The area was fully illuminated. With the back of his hand Fattah slid his glasses up the bridge of his nose and took another close look. Then he started to cut the ragged edges of tissue with the surgical scissors.

The girl bit down hard on her lip and moaned in pain. Her forehead was bathed in sweat. Fattah pushed the flashlight aside with his elbow and said, 'I don't need it anymore.'

Then, rummaging through the contents of the steel tray with the tip of his finger, he said, 'Give me some suture thread.'

At the same time, he glanced at the girl out of the corner of his eye and said coldly, 'It's almost over now.'

The girl moaned again. 'I've already given you two injections of local anesthetic,' Fattah scolded. 'You should be able to put up with this little bit of pain!'

The girl burst into tears. 'But, Doctor, you don't understand . . . it's like . . .'

Fattah spread his hands. 'That's just how it is! Besides, I'll bet you weren't feeling any pain when you—'

Then, stopping himself from saying anymore, he looked up at the ceiling, and said, 'God forgive me.' He turned to the girl and gave her a look of sympathy shot through with sexual desire. He nodded his head slowly for a few moments.

Outside the room, in a dimly lit corridor, two elderly women sat together on a narrow metal bench looking anxiously toward the closed door of the surgery. The one who appeared older, and who kept her face more tightly covered than the other woman, briefly rearranged her chador. She sighed and said to her companion, 'Mehri dear, say a prayer. *Who Answers the Distressed* blessing would be good . . . it'll pass the time so quick, you won't know it!'

Mehri, who was around forty-two, rocked her body back and forth gently, like a mother lulling her child to sleep. As she swayed, a murmured prayer emerged from her lips. As though in mourning, she kept her head down and her eyes fixed on the grimy tiles lining the corridor. Suddenly the girl shrieked from behind the door. Mehri jumped up and stared in terror at her companion. Nearly in tears she asked, 'What are they doing to her, Batul?'

Her voice broke. Batul stroked her back soothingly, and Mehri clasped her face in her hands. Batul took one of her hands in her own. 'It's nothing, my dear, nothing,' she said. 'It's almost over!'

As if all the strength had left her body, Mehri slumped over and moaned, 'It's been a half an hour since they brought her in, and my heart is in my throat, Batul!'

'Fine, but don't you remember what he said? It takes half an hour just to bandage a wound, but hers is a big operation, isn't it?'

Mehri put one hand over the other. 'I'm just afraid they'll do something in there that will maim her for life.'

Batul sneered at her. 'What! Maim her? Doctor Fattah knows what he's doing; you've no idea what he can do. He just has to touch a patient and she'll recover. You'd be amazed!'

This seemed to calm Mehri. She closed her eyes and began to rock back and forth again, making that same soft, high-pitched sound. After a few moments her expression lightened, and she felt a spiritual peace, as if the gates of heaven were open to her.

Mehri and Batul were close neighbors. They kept nothing from each other, not the smallest thing. They never missed their Thursday-night visit to the holy Jamkaran. They would arrive in the early evening and, after saying their prayers and tearfully begging forgiveness from the saint, they would get back to Tehran at night. They told each other their problems, which was how the only person who knew Shahrzad was not a virgin was Batul. Batul, of course, was a good-hearted soul as well as practical. She was the one who had found Dr. Fattah, and, more importantly, got the money to pay his fee. She got it from Mirza, an old man to whom Batul was devoted, without having to say why she needed it. She had told him that it was for a Muslim, a believing soul who needed it to save her honor. That was all.

She took it from him and gave it straight to Mehri without keeping a penny for herself.

Fattah cut the thread with the scissors and handed them to the nurse. 'Finished!' he declared.

He puffed out his chest as though he had just won the Battle of Austerlitz. The girl opened her eyes and answered him with a feeble smile. As he removed his gloves, Fattah waggled his head and said, 'Done a lot of vaulting, have you?'

The girl nodded earnestly.

'Climbed your share of walls and trees, right?'

The girl nodded again.

Fattah brought his head closer and said in a mischievous, jokey way, 'Go tell that to your dear auntie!'

The girl looked at him self-righteously. This time, without sarcasm, Fattah said, 'When did you say the marriage was to be?'

'They've just started the negotiations,' moaned the girl.

'Meaning?' he said.

'At least two or three months,' the girl murmured.

The doctor paused for a moment and thought. He asked, 'What was the rush, then?' He brought his face closer to the girl's again and in a low voice said, 'You'll have to behave for all that time!' Then he snorted. The girl just stared at him innocently.

Fattah pulled away from her and, as if he had just smelled something foul, wrinkled his nose. 'Don't look at me like that!' he snarled. 'This wasn't the first time, or the second. It's obvious from the shape. Don't pretend you're so innocent!'

The nurse was happy to hear Fattah giving the girl such a hard time, and she nodded in agreement at everything he said. When the girl's eyes fell on her, she scowled and turned her nose up to show her disdain—as if she herself were as pure as the driven snow.

The door opened, allowing light to stream into the hallway. Batul and Mehri hurriedly got to their feet and pulled themselves together. Batul said, 'Great job, Doctor! May the Lord reward you!'

Mehri tilted her head and asked, 'How is she, Doctor?'

Like all doctors—in fact, like any important person—Fattah was in a hurry and said impatiently, 'She's fine; just keep your daughters away from places they don't belong.'

Mehri looked at the doctor with annoyance and then hung her head in shame. The doctor said, 'I'll be waiting for you upstairs.'

Fattah opened a small door on the other side of the hall and went up a narrow stairway. On the floor above was a well-lit space, an all-day clinic full of the smell of alcohol, the sounds of creaking beds and groaning patients.

Dr. Fattah was a skilled and charitable physician who, rather than working in a fashionable uptown clinic, stitched up the rips and tears in his patients and retrieved the honor of their families. He worked in a cramped, underground office with a ceiling only half a meter higher than street level, off one of the alleys in the city center, with squat windows that the wind rattled all autumn long. God knows how many girls he saved from the evil of lost virginity in return for three hundred thousand tumans. A 'hymenoplast' famed throughout Tehran, he pronounced the term with such a thick American accent that you'd think he'd completed a course of advanced surgical training in the United States. Lots of girls had said benedictions for him: the girls who were careless when jumping over the ditches beside the road, climbing trees, mounting bicycles—there was no end to the disasters that befell them! And suddenly you'd see they'd . . . He was not that strict about his fee, knowing that someday everybody would be six feet under with only a shroud to their name. That was why he worked with people; but he didn't let it be known from the start, otherwise they'd all want him to do the job for free. It was, all told, because of his helping hands that he had made a name for himself. In all Tehran, from Revolution Street to every part of the city, it was known that there was one doctor with principles, and that was Dr. Fattah.

Not many knew that fifteen years earlier he had been an orderly, but now: well, he ran his own clinic, a charity with ten or twelve young doctors at his beck and call. With medical colleges opening in every corner of the country, a constant stream of graduates entered the job market, making doctors as common as cow dung, and Fattah opened his clinic to any young doctor who came along. They wouldn't ask for a high salary, something of the order of what a plumber or an electrician would make. He liked to see a bunch of doctors working under him. He was thrilled when they bowed and scraped before him. Of course, he would guide them in the practice of medicine, having been around the block a few more times than they had. When he saw them *Doctor, Doctor*ing, running after him begging for financial help or leave, every part of his body would fill with pleasure. At such times he would grow smug and stare at them arrogantly until the last vestiges of their pride and self-confidence were crushed. Then, like any super-important person with a child blocking his path, he would wave his arms, and, with a forced smile, say nonchalantly, 'You again? What is it this time, my friend?'

Trembling with fear, the young doctor would say, 'If you'd be so kind . . . I'd like several days' leave.'

In the intervening silence, Fattah would scowl, reducing the young doctor's resolve to putty.

'You've just come back from leave!'

The young doctor would hasten to say, 'No, Doctor, that was three, four months back!'

'Can't it wait until next week?'

'No, Doctor, my mother back in the village is ill. There's nobody to give her her injections.'

'How many days?'

'Five.'

'It can't be more than three; bring me the slip and I'll sign it.'

While doing these favors Fattah seemed to crow like a rooster, and he would scratch his double chin. Then he would turn his head slightly in the young doctor's direction.

The young doctor would shift his feet, getting ready to try and convince Fattah to grant him the five days, but Fattah would cut him off, saying, 'Quickly now, my friend, I've got work to do!'

Then he would stare unfeelingly at the young man, waiting for him to reply. These stares had a petrifying effect; they were the stuff of terror.

Sometimes they would ask him for an advance, 'Twenty thousand tumans?'

Fattah would grimace and say, 'Money doesn't grow on trees, son . . . Ten thousand's enough for you! Go and write out the slip and I'll sign it. Run along now, I've got work to do!'

He always had work to do. He was always dragging a black leather briefcase with him, which, naturally, was filled with super-important documents. Barrel-chested, with a short neck, he would march around smartly with long strides, and, naturally, to reduce the intensity of his insufferable self-regard, a kindly smile would play across his lips. But this only served to inflate his conceit, which, of course, was something he was aware of.

Fattah closed the door to his office behind him and went to a washbasin. He was washing his hands when someone knocked on the door.

'Who's there?'

It was Mehri; Fattah told her to come in. She opened the door and entered, closing the door behind her. She stood there with her face clenched in her chador and her chin down. 'Sit,' said the doctor.

Mehri sat. Fattah turned off the faucet and took a filthy, threadbare towel from the metal prong on the wall and, as he dried his hands, went behind his desk and sat down. Then he said, 'Well?'

He smiled and stared at her, wide-eyed. Mehri quickly pulled the envelope with the money from her chador.

Fattah glanced at the envelope and then at Mehri. 'Well?' he said again.

Mehri put the envelope on the desk before Fattah and then slid it forward. Fattah tossed the towel on the desk, picked up the envelope, and, without thinking, weighed it in his hand.

'How much?' he asked.

Mehri looked down at the floor and mumbled, 'A hundred and fifty.'

Fattah pursed his lips. He put the envelope on the desk and slid it back toward Mehri.

'What did I say? That won't do!'

Mehri was at a loss and said, 'Doctor, I beg you! We're living hand to mouth!'

Fattah looked at the ceiling, swiveled in his chair, and said, 'Here we go again!'

Then, leaning forward on the desk, he said, 'Dear lady, why can't you understand plain language?'

'But . . .'

'Try to see what I'm saying! Because you begged and pleaded so much, I agreed to the price; otherwise I wouldn't touch it for less than three hundred.'

'Then give me a couple of days to get the rest,' the woman said, on the verge of tears.

Fattah put the envelope in his desk drawer and said, 'I'll give you till the end of the week.'

The woman got up. She bent her head humbly and said, 'God preserve you!'

Fattah made a gesture of dismissal with his hand and said, 'She's not to move for a week. I mean it: absolute rest!'

The woman said, 'God bless you!'

She was still in the doorway when Fattah said, 'I told her to rest for twenty minutes. Then you can take her home.' He added, 'Leave by that door!'

The woman hesitated and looked at him, puzzled. Fattah said, 'The nurse will show you where, ma'am.'

11

It was like any other fall in Tehran, when the city desperately gasped for fresh air after the long summer days of heat and suffocation. But now there was a stiff, dry breeze blowing from the east, which, in addition to breaking up the turgid mass of greasy air, would howl and whirl through the battered alleys and lanes, coating passersby in dust and debris, and nearly uprooting the bare trees found here and there along the gutters. The wind would stop just before the trees broke, but then it would gather strength again, gradually robbing everyone of all patience.

Across from where Fattah parked his car, the house was shrouded in black cloth. Low murmuring and the sounds of mourning came from the wide-open door. Over the doorway was a banner with big letters extending congratulations and condolences to the family and relatives of a war martyr. Fattah stopped for a moment, watching people come and go. All of a sudden they turned on the lights in a portable shrine and everyone sent up prayers to heaven. Fattah came closer. There were two pictures hanging on a mirrored column: one was a framed picture of a haggard old man and the other of a youth, jubilant and victorious; but the two of them looked exceptionally alike. Was it two people who had died? Were they father and son? Fattah read what it said under the pictures. No, only one person had died. All of thirty-five years of age, one soldier, victim of a chemical attack. Two pictures: one taken at the start of the war, the other at the end.

Fattah placed his black leather case in the backseat and sat behind the wheel. Then he spotted them in the thick cloud of dust stirred up by the wind. They were walking away. The girl was staggering as the other two women clad in black supported her under her arms and walked with her step by step. They paused occasionally, probably to allow the injured girl to catch her breath, and again . . .

With a crooked smile Fattah started the car, put it in gear, and drove. He wasn't going very fast, and, as he watched them, he got an idea. When he reached them, he braked to a near halt and honked the horn.

Mehri bent down. Fattah said, 'You should have called a cab! That way . . .' Then he said, 'Get in and I'll give you a lift.'

They turned slightly toward the car; her pale profile was like a painting.

Mehri said, 'That would be too much trouble for you, Doctor. It's not far to our house.'

Fattah said impatiently, 'Get in.'

The women obeyed. Mehri got in first, followed by the girl. Batul closed the door and said, 'May God reward you!'

The car took off and the women settled into their seats.

He looked at the girl's face with her long lashes and sunken cheeks framed in the rearview mirror. *Who did she look like, this one? Oh, God!*

Fattah said, 'Where's your house?'

'After the crossroads, the second alley, but on the other side of the street,' said Mehri.

Fattah laughed, 'So, we're like neighbors!'

Then the girl raised her eyelids to see the possessor of the two eyes fixed on her so brazenly in the mirror. A passage from a book she had snuck home came to mind: *The man undressed the woman with his eyes.*

Fattah's heart sank in fear after he realized why he was anxious. Only one individual had those eyes, the same person who had been Fattah's love all those years, yet whom he had never possessed. *But I had already forgotten her.*

As soon as he said this to himself, the memory that had turned his youth into a perpetual burning opened like an old wound, and suddenly he realized the futility of it.

The narrow street was filled with exhaust fumes, the screams of children, car horns, and the clamor of people. Cars were moving in no particular order, scattered on the street like a regiment of escaping soldiers. No one paid any attention to the lines painted on the sidewalk or the tilting street signs, uselessly installed along the curb.

Cars would try to pass one another on all sides, motorcycles veered this way coming and the other way going, and all at once there was a car coming on Fattah's right trying to make a U-turn in front of him. Taken by surprise, Fattah slammed on the brakes, sending the women flying on the backseat. Fattah let out a stifled curse followed by a *Lord forgive me*; then he smiled in the rearview mirror at the women.

This was driving etiquette in the city: the sudden braking; the obscenity launched from the driver's window; and the response, just as obscene, albeit not returned with full force. It made little difference in the pandemonium caused by the pedestrians, who had been driven onto the street from the sidewalks—which belonged to the peddlers, with their cloths spread on the ground, and their customers.

Fattah looked again, and again those same eyes, at once modest and innocent, now suddenly agitated and heated, sent a thrill through his entire body. He scratched his chest vigorously, arousing himself, getting high.

Shahrzad suddenly sensed she had seen the man before; the face was familiar! But where? The memory came from some faraway place, from a time before she was born.

Mehri said, 'You can stop here, if it's not too much trouble . . .'

Fattah slowed the car, saying, 'Let me turn around and get you to the other side!'

Mehri said, 'Don't bother; walking a few extra steps is nothing.'

Fattah smiled, ignoring the woman's polite gesture, and made a U-turn around the divider. The two women sitting on either side of the patient looked at each other, surprised by this unexpected show of kindness. Mehri said, 'We've been a bother!'

Then, along with Batul, she nodded, affirming what she had said.

Fattah now saw her profile. The girl was looking out of the window, and it seemed like the warm breath coming from her lips was spreading through the closed air in the car. 'At the beginning of the alley, if that's okay with you,' said Mehri.

Fattah slowed almost to a halt and looked down the alley. 'I'm taking you right to your doorstep!' he declared.

Mehri said, 'No, I beg you, for God's sake!'

But he had turned around. Then he said, 'You mean it's impossible for a person to have a cup of tea at your house?'

Fattah laughed, relieving the tension. The women allowed themselves to laugh, and Mehri said, 'Anytime, Doctor!'

Then she looked at Batul out of the corner of her eye. The ambivalence in her expression didn't last a moment; the muscles in her jaw stiffened and, not knowing what all this meant, she turned away. Mehri all at once swallowed her smile.

'Right here, if it's no trouble. We're here!'

Fattah pulled over and stopped. As the women moved to get out, Fattah felt the warmth of the girl's breath on his neck and earlobes, and suddenly he felt himself getting excited. He closed his eyes.

'Thank you, Doctor!'

The voice had a silvery echo. Fattah opened his eyes and bent his head; the warm waves of its colorful, liquid aura receded into the distance.

Just before Mehri closed the door, Fattah said, 'You don't need to bring me the rest!'

Fattah said it in a low voice, as if he was speaking to them from some other world.

Mehri gave him a confused look. Without turning around, Fattah raised his eyebrows and said, 'The rest of the money, I'm talking about!'

He said it so sincerely and with such kindness, you'd think he wasn't aware of his own unprecedented generosity. He put the car in gear. Her hand still on the handle of the open door, and still dazed, Mehri said, 'But . . .'

Fattah's eyes sparkled. Then a moment later he bent his head and looked through the windshield at the girl. She was frowning sweetly as her mother kept her eyes on her. A sudden and pleasant arousal once again coursed through Fattah's veins. Then he said, 'I'm off!'

He looked at Mehri, waiting for her to close the door.

Mehri said, 'This is not right; the least we can do is give you that cup of tea.'

Fattah said, 'Fine. Later! I'll take a rain check. There's plenty of time.'

He didn't wait; turning the wheel, he made a U-turn. Peering from the cracks in their doors and from behind their windows, many of the neighbors saw that a new, foreign car had let Mehri and Shahrzad out at their doorstep. Then they craned their necks to watch until the last moment when the back window of the car, which was filled with the dark reflections of walls and people, moved off into the distance. What was this new car doing in the narrow alley?

His eyes still sparkling, and with that same crooked smile on his lips, Fattah, before turning into the street, looked in the mirror as the three women passed outside the rusted metal gate of their ramshackle home and watched him disappear. Finally, they turned around and entered their home.

Then the gate closed.

2

Fattah turned off the shower and stood motionless for a few moments in the stall. He wiped the beads of water from his arms, shoulders, chest, and belly. Then, opening the shower curtain, he stepped out. Hands on hips, he squinted, looking around for the clock on the wall. He had arrived a half-hour early.

Every Saturday at five was his regular meeting with Aziz and Keramat in the sauna. It was a cozy place, and the other customers were, of course, all familiar with one other. He passed through the lobby and went up to the bar, ordered a drink from Nader, and sat on a stool. The light from recessed fluorescents was magnified by the marble countertop of the bar.

The air was pleasantly humid. Coming from under the door opposite the bar was a mist that crept over the cold, naked tiles, constantly forming folds, layer upon layer, and dissolving in the glowing corners. But any sound had an echo—even the smallest sound—and these were the predominant features.

The stones, tiles, silence, lights, dark corners, and arched ceilings were clearly there. From time to time water would drip down, breaking the silence and conveying a hidden anxiety. Appearing briefly from behind the wavy curtain of moisture were those big, dark pupils. Fattah felt a chill, and goosebumps all of a sudden formed on his skin.

The main character of his adolescent fantasies was a woman, always a woman. His sexual awakening and that pleasant glow, which would pass through his veins like a warm current . . . His mouth filled with thick saliva, which he ladled away with his tongue. He closed his eyes.

They were still there now, but with an unmistakable direct-ness, and they were coming toward him. Somehow the closer they got, the farther they moved away from him; but they kept coming nonetheless.

That small courtyard with its pool of water, which always gave off a foul smell and had several large black fish. The two dark, adjoining rooms, their common wall covered in pictures of her. In one of the pictures, she wore a fedora slightly askew, the way the tough guys did in the movies, and stuck out that juicy round ass; in another . . . They didn't have a television, and when she appeared on the screen, the neighbor's boy would give a wolf whistle, which brought Fattah there in the blink of an eye. When he saw her, it took his breath away. He stood before the television, panting. When he got home, he went straight to the bathroom, closed his eyes, and, seeing her eyes, lips, and neck in his imagination, he leaned against the wall, put his hand between his thighs, brought out his pecker, and, with eyes without pupils, extinguished that maddening, breath-robbing arousal.

He had bought all her tapes. Once he read in a scrap of a newspaper delivered by the wind to their home that the great singing star of Iran would be giving a concert at an uptown cabaret. The paper also had the number for reserving tickets.

The tickets were expensive, more than the cost of a suit and a good pair of shoes. He got the money together and went, but they wouldn't sell him a ticket. They took one good look at him and said, 'This is no place for the likes of you!'

He turned and left. There was a burning in his chest, and all at once he started to run; but the thing he was trying to escape stayed with him, and, a couple of blocks away, he had to stop because he could run no further. He was burning with despair and rage. He closed his eyes and began to bang his fists against a wall, pummeling it so hard and howling so much every passerby, man and woman, young and old, stopped to watch. A guard appeared and sent him away. The wounds still stung, however; he never forgot them—no, never forgot.

But several years later a miracle occurred. He saw her. Everything was like a dream, it happened so suddenly. At that time he was working for Aq Ebram Mohseni, delivering alcohol to customers who had ordered by phone. Where was the address? He didn't remember. Was it Zafraniyeh? Elahiyeh or Niavaran? It was the end of July, and, as the sun beat down mercilessly on the city, he suddenly found himself in the middle of a small paradise, one of those tiny Edens tucked away in the heart of the great hell that was Tehran.

In the midst of a shaded garden, under a sky of an impossibly beautiful blue, on a broad and charming lawn, more gorgeous that the ones he had seen in films or that he had fantasized about in the dark, limited recesses of his imagination, there was a large pool with a diving board and two sizeable kayaks. The kayaks, one orange, the other lemon yellow, were ablaze in the light from the sky and from the water, as they floated upon a heat haze of sunshine and dew. Whenever he blinked, he imagined the kayaks were coming closer to him. Objects appeared to ripple and shimmer as they hovered in the air above the ground.

Several men and women, dressed in bathing suits, were sitting in the shade of a gazebo by the pool, playing cards. Their raucous, uncontrollable laughter made Fattah smile. This was an exceptional moment when it seemed as if their delight was his; the feeling was real, a rare experience.

But there was one, only one, person swimming in the pool. She would raise her head from the water and take a breath and, before the splash made by her head subsided, she dipped under again with an elegant turn. The motion of her arms cutting through the water made a small wave, nothing of which remained but a few bubbles when it met the walls.

A young man had taken away the liquor bottles, and Fattah stood under a tree waiting for them to bring the money. He watched the woman swimming laps in the pool, and, with each lap, he moved a step closer. Then someone suddenly called out to her, and, like one of those autumn moons that goes in and out of the clouds during the nights of insomnia of adolescence, she glided over, straightened her arms, and came out of the water. The pool all of a sudden lost its luster.

If he hadn't heard her name, he probably wouldn't have believed it was her: Googoosh! She approached the people sitting under the gazebo. She bent down and kissed one of the men on the cheek. Then she looked around—for a chair, no doubt—glanced round a second time, and then had no choice but to sit on the man's lap.

Fattah couldn't remember when he was given the money, when he sat on the motorcycle, or when he got to Aq Ebram's liquor shop. He was still in a daze that night when he came home. He spent hours looking at the color posters on the wall. Then he frantically took off his trousers, and, still upright, with his eyes fixed on the pictures, jerked off. This went on for a couple of years, and he would say: *So who's going to fuck 'em, after all!*

That day when he returned to the liquor shop, the first words out of his mouth were: 'I finally saw her, Aq Ebram!'

He pointed to the picture on the wall. The red lips, that black hair, that look, stunning and shameless. Aq Ebram automatically turned and looked behind him; then he opened his eyes wide and asked incredulously, 'Are you kidding?'

After a brief pause, Fattah nodded, and his face gradually became that of a runner who had left all the competition in the dust. It was a chance victory that, when you looked more closely and thought about it, was more of a defeat. Aq Ebram looked at the picture again, and then, suddenly, his blood boiling, stepped back and gave Fattah a swift kick in the ass. For good measure he let out two choice curses and roared, 'Where the fuck were you that it took so long, you little bastard! It's night already!'

Still roaring, and looking at the picture in such a way that you couldn't tell what was going through his mind, he kicked him in the ass again, then again . . .

Aq Ebram had kicked him so many times that whenever he recalled it, Fattah would automatically reach down and rub his backside, which still smarted. Every time he passed by him, Aq Ebram would, for no reason, give him another swift kick; Fattah was shocked, and a shooting pain would cause his guts to knot up and make whatever was in his stomach reach into his throat. In the confusion of the Revolution, on that very first day, when they were setting fire to the liquor stores, he threw the first stone at the huge pane of glass in the front window; the loud, cracking sound it made when it shattered sounded like gunfire at the start of a battle. Aq Ebram stood in his store, beating himself on the head. They took the bottles one by one from the display case and off the shelves and smashed them against the sidewalk. They exploded with popping noises, and the foaming liquid inside them swept the shards of glass along the sidewalk into the drainage ditch by the road. The area reeked of alcohol for a week. In later years, whenever he remembered the incident, Fattah was filled with regret, mourning the loss of the Johnny Walker, the champagnes, and the white French wines.

'How come you're here early this time?'

It was Keramat. Fattah still hadn't turned when Aziz emerged behind him from the locker room.

'The shits don't even call to see whether we're alive or not . . .'

Aziz rubbed the area around his navel and looked at Fattah with his eyes narrowed, as if he were threading a needle. Then he shuddered, with a touching unselfconsciousness. Fattah said irritably, 'I *did* call; you weren't home!'

Then, raising his glass, he shut his eyes and downed his drink in one gulp. He kept his eyes closed for a few moments, as if, by focusing on the passage of the whiskey down his throat, he could intensify its effect. Then there was the sound of running water; Aziz was in the shower, and emerging from the spray came his booming voice, 'Do tell!'

Fattah turned halfway toward the sound of the voice and looked at the faint outline of Aziz's body through the watery shower curtain. He brought the empty glass to his lips again, nodded, and slowly, his eyes transfixed, searched for the thread of his dreams among the folds of steam that, along with the water, came out from under the curtain.

On the curtain was the scene of a reed bed with a full moon shining in a way that made no sense, and a shack with two windows deep in the background; the things in the picture had no shadow, and the images would go in and out of view in the constantly furling steam cloud; but, despite all this, he imagined that they were moving.

Keramat started to sing, as he usually did when he took a shower. In his songs there were always a narrow alley and the whooshing of water, and, of course, the moonlight and the taste of the earth and the chivalrous man in love—with lots of sacrifices—the stuff of popular, classical poetry.

Fattah rotated the glass in his hand and held it up to the light. The sharp edges of the crystalline ice suddenly gleamed in it. 'One more!' he said.

Then he banged the bottom of the glass on the counter. Further away, Nader poured whiskey into an empty glass, measured out the ice and water, and put the drink on the counter before Fattah.

Aziz and Keramat emerged from the shower, dripping wet; with their hair covering their foreheads and eyes, they had the look of innocent children. Keramat said, 'Pour one for us too, will you!'

He swiveled his torso both ways as though exercising, and, thrilled, with his eyes shut, he sighed. He approached the bar, his pampered belly preceding him. Aziz turned his eyes toward the clock on the wall and said, 'Better move it before Hajji comes!'

Hajji always came later than they did, and the boys would get themselves tight before he arrived. Hajji didn't drink. He knew, of course, what they were doing in his absence, but he didn't bring it up, which they put down to his being a gentleman.

Nader placed two more glasses on the counter. Keramat lifted his glass and emptied it before he even sat down. 'Next!' he said.

He sat, making the chair creak under his bulk. Aziz remained standing, wiping water from his body with his palm. Fattah turned toward him saying, 'I swear I called you—two times, even. If you don't believe me, ask your wife!'

Then he gestured with his head and eyebrows to the corner as if Aziz's wife were sitting there. Aziz's tubby upper body began to shake with laughter and, with a confirming nod of his head, said, 'Me, I wasn't there!'

Fattah said triumphantly, 'See!'

Then he searched for someone to witness his victory. A moment later he said, 'Where were you, by the way?'

Aziz furrowed his brow, the furrows arching toward the ceiling; then with a frown and with that same cute, manly gesture, arched his back like a cat caught in opium smoke, and scratched both sides of his arms.

'Abroad?' Fattah asked.

Aziz explained, 'An emergency mission!'

Fattah nodded ambiguously.

Anyone who might cause problems had to be removed from the picture. These cancerous growths had to be cut out with a knife. Aziz did the 'foreign jobs.' They made him responsible for most of the missions outside the country. He had enough knowledge of foreign languages to get himself out of a scrape. He knew his job, and never left anything that could be traced back to them. He would spend a week casing the 'subject,' finish him off, and, before the local police got wind of it, he'd be back in Tehran. His missions came at little cost. The foreign press would raise a stink, the police would issue their reports, they'd be talking about how leads had come in from everywhere; but the ruckus would soon die down. The nation possessed oil and economic power, and so they had friends in every corner of the world!

Sometimes the old comrades would get to talking about the best way to kill off certain people. Should they drag them up a hill and shoot them? Should they hang them from the steel girders of a superstructure, or kidnap them and strangle them in a safe house and dump their bodies in the desert? Or should they be crushed to pieces under the wheels of a truck on some rainy night when the driver was not being as careful as he should? Or should they arrange a confrontation one dark night with a crazy or a drunk, and have their heads smashed in with a lead pipe and their wallets stolen? Fattah had a good head for this type of thing; he would always have some new assassination plan up his sleeve: an injection of alcohol in the arm, or a heart attack induced with a potassium suppository—of course, the nitroglycerin suppository was also effective! That method ensured the entry wound would not be detected. It was his method, and it had been used on various people to good effect. But when an example had to be made for others, he would chop the victim's body into pieces and put them in a freezer, or perforate them with a dagger and dump the body in the wastelands around Tehran.

Nader replaced the empty glasses with full ones. Fattah took Nader's pen from the breast pocket of his white robe, slid the coaster from under his glass, folded it, wrote *Googoosh* on it, and held it for a moment where Aziz could see it. Aziz squinted and read what he had written; then he looked at Fattah, who had put the pen back in Nader's pocket.

Aziz said, 'So . . .?'

Fattah crumpled the coaster, put it in an ashtray, and said, 'Find her for me!'

The way he said it was a little like the way people talk who are in distress, when it's a matter of life and death.

Aziz began turning his glass with the tips of his fingers again, wrinkled his brow, and shrugged his shoulders indifferently. Then he took a gulp and stared expectantly at Fattah out of the corner of his eye.

Fattah said, 'I want her!'

Then he leaned back and filled his chest with air. Aziz lifted his glass from the counter, passed it from hand to hand for a good while, and moved bluish pieces of ice around on the crystalline divider. He said, 'Who for?'

Fattah immediately leaned forward and said, 'For myself!'

His tone was emphatic, suggesting it was his right, and that he would not rest until he got her.

Keramat raised his eyebrows, sipped at his whiskey, and, his eyes two slits, stared pensively at the counter. He was silent, not interfering; it had nothing to do with him. The truth was that all this fuss about love and loving was old hat; in his world, if there was a woman, it was Tala. No woman ever born could tantalize a man like Tala. He had lost her, and whenever he remembered that great mistake of his life, he would hold his head in his hands and sigh.

Aziz said, 'As you know, I work in the foreign section.'

'Yes,' said Fattah, 'ask around; ask the other guys!'

Aziz stared at the counter and then at the glass. He emptied the contents, wiped his mouth with the back of his hand, and smacked his lips. With Fattah still staring at him, he said, 'But, after all . . .'

Fattah interrupted him. 'From the time I was just a little kid, this daughter of a whore . . .'

Without meaning to, he began to tear up. Aziz looked at him and said sympathetically, 'So how come now, after all these years?'

Fattah shook his head restlessly, filled with yearning.

Aziz put his big mitt on his wrist and said, 'If you want quick results, you should go and see Mashallah!'

Fattah said, sneering, 'Mashallah? You know I haven't been to see him in quite a while.'

Aziz said matter-of-factly, 'Fine, so now you go see him!'

Fattah said, 'I don't know where he is.'

Aziz smiled wryly and said, 'Everybody in the bazaar knows him; you go in through the Sabzeh Meydan entrance, then hit the small arched bazaar, and it's right at the entrance to the Imamzadeh Zeyd shrine.'

Whether their conversation had reached an end or not, they stopped, having gotten word from the locker room that Hajji had arrived and was about to disrobe. Nader hastily gathered up the whiskey glasses and poured non-alcoholic beers for them. The sauna was the only place Hajji didn't bring his bodyguards with him. They sat in the car, waiting at the entrance.

He entered the lobby with a towel over his shoulder. The boys got to their feet and greeted him. He waved in acknowledgment and went into the shower.

He deliberately avoided looking at anything much, was monosyllabic, keeping withdrawn and serious. When he did speak, he was terse and wouldn't wait for a response from people, but would turn around and go. But there was one thing he'd always say to them: 'If the Westerners and those lackeys of the West say bad things about you, you should conclude you are doing your duties well, and never hanker for the world's riches. Everybody's going to end up six feet under, no matter what.'

But the time in the sauna was a bit different; the reserve was still there, of course; but this was one of those days when he was less serious, in more of a joking mood, even to the point of making up dirty nicknames for the boys: Aziz was 'Rooster-ass' and Keramat was 'Cow-killer.' Such things were beyond Fattah, so he never had a nickname.

He came out of the shower, locked his fingers together, raised his arms, and brought them behind his back. He arched his body forward, then stretched his back in two directions and, with his customary reticence, shuffled as slowly as possible over to the boys. They bowed to him again, and he sat down. His face had white stubble, bushy eyebrows that spilled onto his eyelids, and a broad snout with three strands or so of thick black hair growing from the end of it. On his arm was the faint, purplish outline of a tattoo, which mostly resembled a woman whose curly locks draped both sides of her face and fell on her shoulders. But on his chest was the image of a crown, on top of which, instead of a row of price-less gems, were random outcroppings of fleecy white hair.

3

Keramat, his eyes still shut, rolled over and yawned. He rubbed his face, moved his jaws from side to side, and stretched. Then he punched the pillow and sighed in deep satisfaction.

The sun poured through the etched glass windows and the lace curtains, bathing the large, pleasant room with an even light. Things were stripped of their artifice in that glow; the floral pattern in the carpet, seeming to sprout from the ground, quivered as though alive.

Ghoncheh opened the door a crack and asked, 'You're still asleep?'

She entered the room and, with her mouth agape, said, 'Get up, already!'

Keramat opened his eyes briefly and said, 'Leave me alone!'

Then he groaned in a deep voice. Ghoncheh sat on a corner of the bed and, as if trying to placate a bratty child, said, 'You told me yourself to wake you at seven.'

'Lay off, will you!' said Keramat.

Ghoncheh stared at her husband testily for a while, and then, hands on hips said, 'So don't ever tell me to wake you up in the morning, okay!'

She turned away in anger, and was about to get up when Keramat reached out and grabbed her wrist and pulled her to him; all at once the couple of kilos of gold hanging from Ghoncheh started to jingle, and, before she could exhale, Keramat had her between his thighs. Ghoncheh was tongue-tied, unable to do anything but gaze at the door in a stupor of delight and say, 'Oh God, the kids!'

A moment later, her panties flew from Keramat's finger into the air, and, like a ceiling bulging with rainwater, he landed on the woman, making the bed creak.

Keramat came once, but, still not finished, started again; he was just warming up. Individual beads of sweat pricked the golden skin of his body, and the musty smell of his slick muscles wafted into the air. Ghoncheh howled with laughter under the man's bulk, and, afraid that the kids might barge in, occasionally looked toward the closed door; but the earthy perfume of the man's body and the welcoming plumpness of his warm belly sent her reeling again.

Keramat's cheeks were still full when he scooped out the last of the cream from the crystal bowl with a lump of flatbread. He was holding the piece to his mouth when the car honked. He shoved it in with his fist and moved it around under the millstones of his jaws, and, finally, swallowed the lump prematurely; the veins in his neck popped out, his eyes bulged and filled with tears, and beads of sweat formed on his forehead. He turned away, gasped and, as though just learning news of some catastrophe, declared, 'They're here!'

Ready with another piece in her hand, Ghoncheh looked joylessly at the kitchen window and said, 'Finish your breakfast now!'

She gave him the bread, shifted her hips, and went to the window. She opened the curtain a crack and muttered, 'Can't they ever let him finish his damned breakfast in peace!'

Keramat put the lump in his mouth, picked up a glass of tea and gulped down half of it; tea spilled from his lips. Ghoncheh ran to the closet, took out Keramat's jacket and, as she always did, brushed it off with her elbow and then held it up. Keramat turned his back to her, dipped his shoulders, and put it on. With one sleeve still flapping, he bent down and put on his shoe; then he put his arm in the sleeve and gave Ghoncheh her spending money for the day. He hadn't finished the bread, which was still going from side to side in his mouth when he said, 'I'll be home late tonight; the boys and I have arranged to go to Hajji's.'

There was a spark of joy in his eyes. When they went 'to Hajji's,' they would sit at his feet, bobbling their heads in such a way that you'd think they were innocent little lambs. He would preach, putting the fear of hellfire into them and getting them ready to serve. Keramat would always say, 'Morale is what we get from Hajji, morale.'

'You mean you're coming home late?' asked Ghoncheh.

She gave him a look that showed her displeasure. She opened the door for him and said, 'Take care of yourself.'

With his back to the woman, Keramat glanced up at the sky and recited a benediction under his breath.

His bodyguard opened the door. Keramat waved and got in. Ghoncheh leaned her head to one side and said under her breath, 'I entrust him to you, O Lord.'

It was not possible to go to work using the same car two days in a row. They were always changing vehicles: Patrols, Benzes with curtains or dark windows, sometimes even

Paykans or Land Rovers, always changing daily. No one knew exactly what he did for a living; many thought that he worked in one of the institutions set up under the Revolution, which was true to a certain extent. Ghoncheh would, naturally, say to the neighbors, 'My husband's an inspector for the slaughterhouse; every day he inspects the butchers in a different part of Tehran!'

Ordinarily they took the special bus lane, which was empty, making contact on the radio with the prison and reporting their whereabouts; but whatever happened, they weren't on the road for more than half an hour. They were waiting for him, so when they arrived, the large metal gate was open.

Evin Prison was on a hill at the foot of the Elburz Mountains, a village with a commanding view of the megacity of Tehran, and strangely silent as a small crowd gathered outside the gate, its high brick walls topped by several rows of barbed wire, adding to their height, and small guard towers at intervals atop high metal supports. Officers armed with rifles pushed the crowd back from the door. Their puzzling and clipped answers satisfied none of the waiting people; all they could expect was not knowing what to do, and more waiting.

The prison was a city in itself. The blocks, full of prisoners, echoed with the patter of feet and constant whispering; in the bare cells the smallest sound would become an uproar; but the sounds that reigned over the prison were the benedictions and dirges for the Holy Imams that issued from loudspeakers twenty-four hours a day.

Block 325 had two sections one after the other off the main road; the block was like a house with tall green trees in the yard. After a steep hill and before you turned, you reached Block 209, which was the women's prison. There was an underground part where prisoners were interrogated and then 'educated' with a length of steel cable. Cries and screams would constantly be heard from that locale. A relatively large cell, covered by a metal screen instead of a ceiling, served as the exercise yard.

Block 216, the newest, had six rooms. It had a brick facade and small arched windows and a marble architrave. On the other side of the main street were two other blocks, which, before the Revolution, were places for education and relaxation. After that was a block that had been the prison infirmary, with five rooms; it now served as the women's wing. Of these six blocks, two belonged to the women, and the rest were for the men, and in all six blocks, but especially in the women's prison, ailments that caused hair to fall out and boils to appear on the skin were epidemic.

There were other buildings in the prison complex that together gave it the look of a mysterious castle. These buildings were devoted to such prison facilities as the administrative and security offices, and even a prosecutor's section, where, on the third floor, Lajvardi had his office, and which, during business hours, was exceptionally crowded. The administrative buildings had pleasant rooms with large windows. There was another hall, a visiting room with a glass partition that divided the prisoners from their visitors.

Evin was empty now. The blocks were quite full in 1981, the year of the upheaval, the year that Bani Sadr was removed from the presidency, and the Mojahedin announced their armed insurrection. Ordinary prisoners were transferred to other prisons to make room for the ones belonging to various political groups. During the street clashes and the raids on the group hideouts, they rounded up many boys and girls, and later, when all of the blocks at Evin were given over to political prisoners, there were forty people to a cell made for three, which meant that there was no possibility of sitting, let alone sleeping. Visiting the prison was like going back to high school, there were so many underage girls. The average age was seventeen, so that when the door to the exercise yard opened, it was like recess.

In 1988 the number of prisoners suddenly went down again; that was the year they cut off all visits and, after several weeks, finally gave each of the parents gathered outside the prison gate a bundle of clothing.

But this is not the whole story of the mysterious castle, not even its entire geography; the prison also had a factory, an exercise room, and a prayer hall, all of which were near the hill. The hill was the same one that, early in the morning, prisoners, moments before their execution, would ascend blindfold, drinking in the pure dawn air with rapid, fitful breaths.

The prison factory had wood and metal shops, where prisoners who were serving out the last years of their confinement, or those well-behaved inmates who, after so many years in limbo, had finally received their definitive sentences, would work making simple objects, which, naturally, found no customers in the bazaar. The prisoners who had avoided the mass executions of 1988 worked there too, laboring happily, thankful for this glorious accident, and waited to be released. On the factory campus there were smaller rooms in which they had set up carpet looms, which the young girls normally operated. Those people who had seen the rug workshops deep in the remote cities and villages of Iran were astonished by the similarities between the two groups of weavers.

Guard towers and armed young men! Under the broiling sun of summer and in the biting cold of winter, they are forever looking at their watches, waiting for their shift to be over, and in their hearts they constantly curse imperialism for deceiving the youth of the nation, who are now serving out their sentences in the common prison blocks or in solitary cells. From atop their towers they also witness countless times deluded, incorrigible youths take their last steps up the steep hill.

In summer, dawn began with the singing of the birds, and in winter, with the awakening of the creatures that scampered across the dry snow and rustled the thin, bare branches of the bushes. If the traces of violence associated with the special architecture of the buildings and the apparatus of a political prison were removed, one would think it the perfect spot for a charming park.

The prison was neighbor to a village, Evin, with an old-fashioned main street, a small bazaar, and a mosque with finials that hummed three times a day with the sound of the muezzin's call. The entryway and interior of the mosque were festooned with colored lights on every occasion, big and small; but now the mosque was completely overshadowed by the prison, and most people who knew anything about Evin knew it because of the prison.

Keramat took his mobile out of his pocket and turned it off. He took another phone from a shelf and, almost before he could turn it on, it rang.

'Yes?'

'. . .'

'I've just arrived, okay, I'm coming . . . just one minute!'

At first, Keramat was in charge of a handful of boys; these boys beat up the girls who sold the political splinter groups' newspapers at traffic lights. Then Mashallah the Butcher promoted him and now he ran a couple of prisons. He was not only in overall charge of both prisons, but also responsible for their revolutionary identity.

He had yet to enter the prison when a whole herd of people ran after him, from the head cook of the prison to the interrogators; they would all say something, and Keramat would only nod and occasionally lift an eyebrow and would turn just a little bit toward each person until he finally reached his office, which was almost full of people. First, he took off his jacket and leaned on the back of his chair; this was his practice whether it was summer or winter. Then he would roll up his sleeves, which may have been an old habit from the time he worked at the butcher's. Then he would say, 'Now, then!' and turn to the throng, and, when they all started speaking at once, he would wave his hands to quiet them and say, 'One at a time!'

Keramat left by the back door, took the steps two at a time, and went to the cellar. The guard opened the door for him, and he entered the hallway.

No one was there now, but for years when he entered he would see swollen legs and feet, bandaged and bloody, belonging to blindfold bastards, leaning against the wall or sitting in wheelchairs, waiting to be interrogated. On the green tiles, in addition to those feet were drops of blood, bits of dry bread, plastic plates and cups, as well as an air of anxiety and savagery, which, like a sticky film that poured from the walls, oozed along the hallway, emitting wave after wave of noxious vapor. Some cried out, some patiently waited, and some even tried to take advantage of the guards' not looking to push their blindfolds back and look around, whereupon there would be a commotion and the sounds of beating after beating.

Keramat opened the door to a room off the hallway and went inside.

It was a small room, which at first glance was in disarray. On a plastic tablecloth covering part of a broad table were pieces of bread, copper plates with bits of eggs sunny-side up stuck to them, a salt cellar, a glass of tea . . . Keramat looked at the table; it was clear they were just finishing breakfast. The two men sitting at the table got to their feet when they saw him and greeted him.

Keramat stepped forward and said, 'Where are they? The ones you were talking about?'

One of the men pointed to the other end of the table. Keramat drew back, squinted, and said, 'What are they?'

The man said, 'They make statues out of the doughy part of the bread!'

Keramat put his hands on his hips and said indifferently, 'Fine, let them make them! Screw 'em!'

The man picked up one of the statues and put it in Keramat's hand. He tossed it in the air once or twice, judging its weight, and then looked at the man, waiting for him to say something. The man said, 'This statue, for example, shows a man with a clenched fist raised above his head.'

Keramat picked up the statue, stared at it and said, 'You mean . . .'

The man said, 'They're using it to keep up their morale!'

Scowling, Keramat yelled, 'Sons of bitches!'

He looked at the statue again, and, rolling it in his palm, said, 'What did you say they're making it with?'

'Bread dough,' said the man.

Keramat said immediately, 'Fine. So don't give them any more dough!'

The man said, 'See, that won't work . . . They make them in Handicrafts and send them out the first chance they get.'

Keramat didn't stay to hear more; he ran all the way to the entrance to the women's wing. When he entered, everybody scattered. Keramat let them have it: 'By the honor of the blessed Fatima, if I see another person going around the ward without a hijab, she'll have me to deal with!'

He got so red in the face it was hard to tell whether he was speaking or spitting, but, whichever the case, the young woman who was standing near him and was prevented from fleeing by his sudden appearance, begged, 'Have a heart, Hajj Aqa, we . . .'

Keramat angrily turned in her direction and, looking at her bare legs, shouted and raised his whip.

The girl shrieked and started to run. Keramat brought his whip down on the tiles and said, 'Stupid bitch!'

Everything went dead quiet. No one had the nerve to breathe. It was as if all the oxygen in the room had been sucked out through Keramat's ample nostrils. Then he began to move.

As he walked before them, they bent their heads and lowered their shoulders, and Keramat puffed out his cheeks and ascended to the heavenly throne. Then he suddenly remembered the Lord, and his double chin quickly deflated till once again his gaze fell upon the hypocrite infidel; then once more he inflated slowly and hovered above the heads of all these poor, weak creatures in their headscarves. This was followed by another sudden descent.

This wasn't a prison, it was a place where they built humans; here was where they ironed out the kinks in them and put them on the straight and narrow. Keramat was certain that, however much he ranted and raved at them, it would be to his credit on Judgment Day, as would the lashes he applied to their backs.

Then he bellowed again, 'Everybody out into the hallway! I'll count to three.'

Once again there was bedlam. The girls began to run, each into a cell to grab something. By the time the next eruption came, they were standing in line against the wall.

He inspected them one by one; all were tightly wrapped in their chadors; then he looked at their feet; some were barefoot, some only had enough time to find one stocking, others were wearing stockings that didn't match. Keramat made a face and laughed sarcastically. The girls were emboldened by this and everyone tittered. Keramat gave them a furious look, and everybody fell silent. Then he inspected the routed army, and at the end of the line, pointing with the whip in his hand, showed his minions their feet and said with a sneer, 'Look at them!'

Another wave of laughter. Keramat yelled, 'Are you going to shut up, or not!'

The laughter died down somewhat but not completely, not until Keramat's next outburst. Then he looked them up and down, trying to humiliate them, and, with his eyes narrowed, said malevolently, 'Now you're going to make a statue of your mommies for me! I want to hand-deliver them to your daddies to remind them what kind of children they've spawned! Got it?'

They were unclean, which had to be brought home to them in a way that made them finally believe it, and then they could repent.

Sparks of anger shot from Keramat's eyes as he searched for the wing leader. He found her and said, 'You stay right here till I'm done with them!'

Then he signaled to his minions with raised eyebrows. A number of them began attacking the cells. Nothing was safe from their assault: they unzipped duffels, spilled out the contents of sacks, tossed boxes in the air, weeded out the unnecessary and suspicious things so they could take them away. A moment later Keramat, fully inflated and ready to fly, exited the wing with his minions. Then, suddenly, all of that pent-up energy was released.

Now there were no more inmates in the wings where he, amazed by the number of infidel women in the land, would parade before them saying, 'So you want to be Lenin's wife, do you?'

Then he would kick them between the legs, and, if they made no sound or movement, he would give them another kick in the exact same spot; then another, stronger than the first two, until finally they would start bleeding and drop to the ground. They could do almost anything to these prisoners, especially after one of the Mojahedin assassinated the warden with a weapon he had taken from his bodyguard.

Keramat had yet to settle down after what he had seen in the women's wing, and was still swearing through clenched teeth when Mostafa came to him saying, 'Come by Solitary Eight.'

Keramat looked at him questioningly. Mostafa explained, 'You told me yesterday to remind you.'

Keramat kept staring, and Mostafa explained further: 'I'm talking about that girl, Manizheh.'

Keramat nodded and changed direction. His minions followed. He kicked the door open with his foot and paused at the threshold.

The young girl was balled up in the middle of the cell with her head between her knees. Keramat came forward and kicked her in the back with the bottom of his shoe. She groaned and rolled on her side, stayed like that for a few moments and then rolled herself into a ball again. Keramat clenched his teeth and nodded, and looked at her as though he were crushing a bug, as though there were a connection between the blows of his shoe and entry to the promised heaven with its seventy houris, all exclusively his, and its streams of milk and honey. It was for this that the blows became harder, but they still didn't soothe him, so he kept on brutalizing her.

Keramat kicked her in the side with the toe of his shoe, making her roll on her side again. Then they looked at each other.

As they did, their mutual hatred thickened, overflowed their eyes, and, like excrement, filled the air in the cell. Keramat stood with his legs apart, and, bringing his hand toward his crotch and directing the heat of his fevered breathing toward the girl, said, 'I'm going to tear your tongue out of your throat, you bitch!'

This in a deep, bruised tone of voice. What underlay that voice was the only thing in the cell that had any vitality.

Again those dirty looks! It was as if every ounce of the young girl's strength had been converted into a lethal rage, which was revealed in her hard stare and rapid breaths. Keramat bent over her, wanting to see her up close. Yes, she was an insect; he was certain of it.

Keramat straightened up and turned to Mostafa, 'Well?'

Mostafa shook his head despairingly, 'Nothing!'

Keramat went on all fours in front of Manizheh, bashed her in the head with his keys, and said, 'You won't leave this cell alive unless you open that stinking mouth of yours!'

He gave her several more bashes with the same set of keys, a heavy set of about fifteen. Then he rose, looked at his minions for a moment, turned on his heel and, as he was leaving the cell, said, 'Corrective punishment.'

The girl shrieked in terror, went into convulsions, and emitted an incomprehensible sound from deep within her lungs. All at once she lost consciousness as if seized by a deep sleep.

Mostafa walked over to Keramat. 'After all the time you've been here, you still don't know how to do your job right, Mostafa!' he said under his breath.

Mostafa opened his mouth as if about to speak, but Keramat tuned away saying, 'Son of a bitch!'

It was his favorite expression, but it wasn't clear at whom it was directed; when he couldn't find something in his pocket, when a door slammed somewhere, when his foot landed in a pothole filled with water, he would say, 'Son of a bitch!'

Mostafa stood in the half-open door of the cell until Keramat and his entourage had left. Then he blew his stack. He savagely turned on the girl and kicked her hard in the ass. The girl screamed and then hawked as if something thick was caught in her throat; finally she let out a pitiful howl, a howl that quickly faded to a constant sob.

Mostafa went up to her again and, as though comforting a child, stroked the girl's anus with the tip of his shoe. The girl continued to whimper, and Mostafa continued to bring his shoe tip in and out. Then, in a particular tone of mouth-watering pleasure, he said, 'Feels good, doesn't it?'

No sound, no movement. Mostafa said, 'It's got to feel good, 'cause you're not talking.'

Manizheh got up from the floor part way and screamed into Mostafa's face. Mostafa slapped her hard and shouted, 'Shut the hell up, you tramp!'

Manizheh sprawled on the ground again and started crying. Mostafa went around the girl and, when he got to the hole in the floor that gave off the cloying stink of urine, gave her another hard kick in the ass.

Then, with foam coming from his mouth and his eyes half closed, he went to the entrance of the cell and called out, 'Where are you, boys?'

A moment later, three or four people came running to the cell and formed a circle around the girl. Mostafa kicked her in the crotch savagely.

One of them sneered, 'Hurt?'

The girl raised her eyebrows, meaning to say *no*. She was telling the truth because her body could no longer feel anything. There was another kick—from whom she couldn't tell, and the same voice said, 'She's a lying bitch; if she didn't feel it, she wouldn't be crying like that.'

The girl suddenly put her hands over her stomach and rolled herself into a ball. She dragged herself on the floor to the latrine hole; the sound of her retching echoed around the wing. Then she made loud hiccuping noises that sounded strangely like fingernails scraping glass.

Mostafa didn't move; he just shook his head in disgust. The greenish liquid the girl had brought up turned his stomach.

4

Khanjan loaded the plate with rice and placed it in front of Mostafa. As she slid the bowl of stew toward him, she said, 'Bon appetit!'

She stared at her son's hands with a mixture of pleasure and fervent hope. Mostafa picked up the bowl and emptied half of it on the rice. Khanjan clasped her hands and, as if suddenly remembering something, said, 'Did you forget it was today?'

Mostafa put the spoon in his mouth and looked at Khanjan. She smiled bitterly and looked back at him in disappointment. His mouth full, Mostafa shut his eyes and said in embarrassment, 'Tomorrow! Absolutely. You can be sure, tomorrow I'll definitely go find her.'

A couple of grains of rice fell from his mouth onto the tablecloth.

Khanjan said, 'You know, darling, Ezzat Sadat took the girl in when she was an orphan and raised her. They say she's quite the young lady! They definitely arrested her by mistake!'

She nodded, confirming what she had said. Mostafa said, 'Swear to God; tomorrow, I promise. Count on it!'

And he shook his fist in the air so forcefully that if she'd been anybody but his mother, she would have believed him.

Khanjan said, 'You only have to sit with her aunt and hear how she raves about the girl! She says that whatever money came her way, it all went for pencils and notebooks, which she gave out to the poor slum kids.'

Mostafa looked at Khanjan out of the corner of his eye and thought better of what he was about to say. He put the spoon in his mouth again.

Khanjan asked, 'You were saying, darling?'

Mostafa chewed the food thoroughly, swallowed, and washed it down with two gulps of water. Then, after hemming and hawing, said, 'I only hope—God forbid!—that she wasn't one of these little Communists, Khanjan!'

'Little whats?' asked Khanjan.

'Little Communists,' said Mostafa. 'Meaning, the atheists! Meaning the ones who can't tell what's permitted from what's forbidden and the legal from the unlawful—their women . . . with all the men. You know!'

Khanjan slapped her leg with her hand, shook herself, then spit between her thumb and index finger, and finally bit her finger. 'For shame! Beg God's forgiveness, sweetheart! It does you no credit running your mouth that way behind the back of a believer!'

Mostafa glanced at Khanjan and said, 'Just kidding—that's all!'

Then he brought another spoonful to his mouth. Vexed, Khanjan rose, groaning from the pain in her legs, but still shaking. In a more serious tone, she said, 'It does you no good to kid that way!'

She left the room, feeling let down.

Mostafa watched her go, and when the door closed, resumed his chewing.

Manizheh Ebrahimi! The girl that said zilch! After all these years, Mostafa had netted a person who the more she was beaten, the less she said, and—what was worse—someone his mother was championing. The girl had spent the first couple of days in the hallway, conveniently available, at hand so that anybody could pick up extra points for the Final Reckoning with a spit or a smack; this was her allotment from people who happened to pass by. By the end of the week a slimy film covered her body, which gave off the yeasty odor of infection like something concrete, but it vaporized, and hovered in the fetid air of the hallway. Doors opening and closing made the air move, and it seemed the smell got worse, perhaps penetrating the skin of the jailers. If not, why was Khanjan always saying to Mostafa, 'Whenever I gather up your bedding, you can't believe how horrible it smells!'

They caught her in the street with a weapon, and, after a month of beatings and cross-examination, they still hadn't gotten anything from her. At the time of her arrest, she wolfed down a piece of crumpled paper. The next day Keramat wanted them to send her shit to a laboratory to find out what was written on the paper. When they told him that no such laboratory existed, he was crestfallen; but he was convinced that the Americans had invented one and were cleverly covering it up. He felt that we should roll up our sleeves; after all, Iran had at long last become self-reliant!

Khanjan returned to the room, and Mostafa, a hidden smile on his face, demanded, 'Well, what's the latest?'

Khanjan nodded uncertainly and looked at her son expectantly; Mostafa's tone was playful. 'There should be news anytime now, right?'

Khanjan suddenly got the point, saying coyly, 'Be patient, darling!'

Mostafa was nagging now. 'How much longer? Tell me! If there's another suitor in the works, you've got to let me know!'

'There isn't,' she said. 'But they say we've got to give them time to think. We're talking about a whole lifetime—it's no joke, sweetheart!'

'You can't give them a ring, or something?' Mostafa asked.

'I have nothing against it, but we'll lose in the bargain!' Then she made a wry face and looked down at the carpet. 'It's as if they've got some beauty queen on their hands! Isn't there anybody who'll tell them what's what? It isn't like we're trying to make a match with some well-heeled family!'

He imagined he saw Shahrzad again, proud and aloof, with those same heavy eyelids half closed; there was a melody to her voice that was both counseling and cautionary at the same time and sent a warm wave through Mostafa's soul.

'Why are you always standing in my way?' she asked. 'I'm not one of *them*, you've got to know that!'

Mostafa looked down, so embarrassed he wanted to sink into the ground; then he turned and left. The girl's modesty and innocence had suddenly penetrated the deepest recesses of his soul; he had, of course, pointed out their home and sent Khanjan to their doorstep.

That evening when she returned, she had news for him. 'They were very hospitable to me. What a mother! I had a ball. What a lady that woman is! She immediately brewed tea. I told her that I just had the one son, who saw your daughter and fancied her. My son, I said, is a responsible family man and, as his mother, I'm very proud of him! No objections. They asked about what you do. I told them that you worked for the state and brought home a decent wage . . . I saw the girl, too—a doll. She sat with us for a few minutes, looking down at the carpet.'

As he chewed his food, Mostafa thought, 'Why should I go out and rent a room from strangers? Mother will be lonely. I'll get a loan and enlarge the second floor; it'll make a good room. How many people are we, after all? What about kids? How many does she want? Let's leave it up to fate. Whatever the Lord wants!'

5

Tehran lay at the foot of the Elburz Mountains like a bloated corpse rotting in the sun. It suffered from the faulty exhausts of its vehicles, the rage of its inhabitants, the dry wasteland to its south, and the sky-high mountains in the north that kept moisture and fresh air from reaching it. The city was filled with passing odors, off-key melodies, cheap entertainment, and minor crimes. The uncovered arroyos that began in the northern heights and descended to the bogs and lowlands at the base of the city conveyed a black sludge filled with greengrocers' waste, sanitary napkins, and watermelon rinds. Trapped along the banks were also old tires, the carcasses of dogs and – if you exclude the sparkle in the eyes of bashful girls – perhaps the only hint of the erotic in the huge city, the white rings of used condoms bobbing helplessly on the water.

The Iran–Iraq war had, of course, ended, and they had renovated the streets and filled the large potholes in the asphalt; where streets met they had cultivated chrysanthemums and violets in huge cement planters—the stems of the flowers drooped, their blooms were soiled, and their leaves yellowed. The cement columns of the flyovers were painted in a nauseating shade of blue. The schools, for their part, were now operating three and four shifts a day, and everywhere you looked the city was brimming with children. Despite its long history, Tehran had never seen such turmoil and affliction.

Smog, noise, smog again; the air was heavy and murky with dirt and dust, redolent with intrigue and vomit, which made the air seem even more sluggish. There were shrieks, cars honking and braking suddenly, and vile curses, which were powered up from the nether regions and dispersed so openly and generously in the leaden atmosphere that everyone got their share. There was constant whispering, forced laughter, filthy jokes about politics, and the customary dread hidden behind people's eyes, like a common habit or sign of heresy, added to the chill in the air and redoubled the feeling of fear.

Fattah was on foot; the streets were clogged with old passenger cars and junky pickups. The bicycles didn't seem to have brakes, their riders continually howling at pedestrians to get out of their way. He proceeded to where the alleys suddenly fanned out from the street. The neighborhood was packed with houses, their copings ragged, gutters broken, with battered metal-stripped doors, shattered bricks, and, here and there, bulges in the walls marked by urination, whose acrid smell was given more substance by the constant perspiration of bodies. Then there were the electric lines, crisscrossing the blue sky and covered in pigeon droppings and soot; air-conditioning ducts; billboards, large shop windows displaying junk from all over the world, junk bathed in the darkish-yellow light of the fluorescent tubes; and counters overflowing with plastic knickknacks. Women in dark garments or chadors wandered aimlessly—more aimlessly than the rest—from the sidewalks to the sides of the streets and back again. Some mysterious force made them all look alike. Even their eyes, the way they moved their arms, and their coughing were all the same. Out of necessity, they stopped once in a while to talk uneasily with one another, and then went on; it was as if the atmosphere were pregnant with the impossible. Not only were they part of the general scene, but surely so was Fattah.

He'd walked these parts during his childhood, but now he didn't seem to recognize them. How far was it to Darkhungah, after all? Before he knew it he was at the old royal residence of Shams al-Emareh; or had he reached the sub-bazaar of Kal Abass Ali and the Passage of Taqi from that direction? Hardly two steps—and he was there!

On Fridays his mother would take him by the hand and bring him to the old city of Robat Karim, where they would visit the old fort or the mausoleum of the cleric Seyyed Malek Khatun, or the Bibi Shahrbanu shrine. Not counting the ordinary chapels and mosques of Tehran, three of the thirty shrines where descendants of the Holy Imams were buried were near their home. His mother, naturally, had the most faith in the shrine of Seyyed Nasroddin; she would visit it and tie threads on the bars of the metal grate around the sepulcher, make her vows, and cry. One time she wasn't wearing socks, and a woman, for no good reason, scolded her: 'You should be ashamed of yourself, coming here barefoot!'

Fakhri, his mother, white with embarrassment, had wrapped herself up tight in her chador, but it did no good; a man came and threw her out of the shrine.

Fattah and his mother also went to the Zeyd shrine as well as the Yahya shrine, which were farther away, and even to the Saleh shrine, which they had to take a bus to reach. On the way back the bus smelled of yogurt, the kind sold in clay pots, and of chicken droppings.

The mosques, with their worn floor coverings, wooden pulpits, and dark niches, filled little Fattah with a special kind of dread that made him burst into tears at the slightest provocation. People there were always saying that sin was a bad thing, punished by hellfire; but avoiding sin was a very, very hard thing to do. He couldn't just ignore the big, open-mouthed jars in Mashdi's Grocery; especially those times he would go there for soapwort or fuller's earth, and Mashdi would go to the back room, and the rock candies would open their mouths and say to him, *Hurry, take us! Quick, before he comes back!*

His mother told him this was Satan speaking.

On Sunday mornings, Fattah would do anything to escape from school in order to go to the Church of St. Thaddeus, which was different from anything else in the city. Once, he was able to enter the enclosure and, hiding behind the bushes in the garden, watch what was going on in the church. How beautiful it was! Directly opposite his hiding place was a niche in the altar with a picture of a woman. The wind had pushed back her chador to reveal her cradling a naked child. Above the altar they had hung the statue of a man, his head resting on his shoulder, his arms outstretched, and blood dripping from his hands and bony feet. He was naked but for a towel wrapped around his loins. Later Hasan Khanom told him that the statue was the prophet of the cross-worshippers, a man the Jews had killed!

People sat on benches in that long room, row upon row, praying and touching their chests, foreheads, and stomachs. At the other end of the room there was a large table covered in red felt. There were some books, and then it was candles almost everywhere, at the entrance, on the steps, all lit. Then the organ sounded, and this was the only place Fattah heard that sound. His mother said they were infidels because even when they prayed they played an instrument. Then she bit her thumb and forefinger, spat, then bit them again and sought forgiveness for her sins.

There was no end to the passion plays he saw: *The Holy Cloak, The Khadijeh, The Qoreysh Wedding*. When the guards got wind of them, they would break up the displays and attack people. The women would hide bits of scenery and props under their chadors, saving them so that the next day the players could reassemble the pieces in the privacy of people's homes.

Fattah turned from the parade grounds at Tupkhaneh Square toward the Homayun Gate. Here and there along the way there were readers, who read for free, standing in front of the newspaper stalls. As he walked on, the scene changed there was a layer of soot on the canvas sunshades, which were once vibrantly colorful. At this point, the shops mostly sold sport coats and pants, coats of indeterminate cut that would save a family's honor because fathers and sons could share them. They were cheap, intended primarily for the village children. The sidewalks here were broader, making it easier to walk, but they were also coated in a layer of mucus hawked up from throats and shot out of nostrils. Naturally the handcarts bearing goods for the market also traveled on the sidewalks, pushed by people constantly huffing and puffing in many accents: Kurdish, Turkish, Rashti, Dari, and Bushehri.

At the corner there were many beggars, some selling the usual packs of gum, others telling fortunes with the poems of Hafez. Many were just kids with rheumy eyes and dirty faces, who would stick to passersby like glue, pestering them to buy what they sold. Some sat by the wall displaying chronic wounds—often bloody—on their legs or shoulders.

Fattah turned into Sur-e Esrafil Avenue, where there were also some clothing stalls. From there, he went to Naser-e Khosrow Avenue, and suddenly, looming above the crowd was the great blue dome!

The crowds were thicker here, everyone hurriedly coming and going, with sweat on their faces, without a smile or a greeting. There was a bicycle-repair shop too, and a store that sold prayer rugs, cloths, Qur'an holders, and Moharram banners, as well as keffiyehs, paramilitary headbands, compasses, and prayer beads. Again there was a small crowd of professional newspaper-readers. He passed in front of Shams al-Emareh and Marvi Alley. The large clock in Shams al-Emareh had stopped, and burly black crows loitered near its pigeon coops. Further on, at the corner of Buzergmehri, motorcyclists shouted out their destinations to potential passengers, making Fattah cover his ears. Next on Buzergmehri came the shops selling salted, roasted nuts and seeds, red lentils, citrons, Tabriz roses, white marshmallows, fresh jujubes, shallots, and sugared orange peels. Fattah, who was deep in thought, found himself at Sabzeh Meydan Square.

Here were shoe repairers and peddlers selling loofahs, birds that talked, and Viagra pills. The country types lounging about leered at the full figures of the city ladies and, with the seat of their pants reaching their knees, the corners of their mouths shone with spittle. Trapped in the tiny particles of air there was a kind of violence that might burst free at any moment. The atmosphere was one of vice and lust, thinly veined with a nauseating stink that came up from the waste streaming in the gutters and from mouths full of rotting teeth and swollen gums. Yes, here it was: Sabzeh Meydan!

Fattah cut through the crowd milling in front of the square and entered the bazaar, stopping for a moment while everything was still dark. He blinked a couple of times, and colors began to materialize, then the goods, which were piled one atop the other in no particular order. Finally his eyes adjusted to the darkness. Thanks, apparently, to the emissions from the old bricks, there was a chill in the closed space, which made the air bracing; nevertheless, the heavy odor of abandonment which seeped into the air from cracks in the mortar added a kind of ancient-eastern lassitude to the atmosphere. Countering that, crooked shafts of light streaming in from the round skylights in the row of domes on the roof of the bazaar shone at regular intervals on the pillar piers and entrances to the cell-like shops, revealing a thick mass of dust particles that, one might imagine, was the main agent of all the chaos.

The bazaar was abuzz with scurrying feet and a monotonous undertone, which, with a nervous laugh, a curse, or an uncivil word, an unfinished greeting or a hasty farewell, would suddenly grow, like the sound of the wind, becoming clear and audible, and, a moment later, echo like a raging torrent in the maze of passageways that ran under the arched ceilings. If not newly painted, they would be awash with pigeon droppings and cobwebs.

Among the soprano and bass sounds and the alternation of light and shadow, people would jostle one another, their hands full, not bothering to apologize. They were beset by a kind of inexplicable disorder. Suddenly there would be the nauseating, low-pitched sound of scraping metal made by the ungreased ball bearings of carts pushed by aged porters, who, yelling and screaming, warned people to get out of their way. It was like a scene out of history, frozen in time, in which, in the dreadful seconds of the climax of a story, the peerless hero falls.

A mixture of odors—the smell of the body-washers, moist earth, sweat, and bodies needing a bath—wafted into the air. There was the acrid smell of urine from the public urinals too, which, like all pungent and impermanent things, hung in the air for a time then disappeared. People by the walls eating soup added the complex aroma of spices and cooked spinach. Odd colors and strange smells, the deep darkness of the recesses, weightless objects and shadows that disappeared . . .

They sold everything in this bazaar, but there were things also that were available at other places. If it was a tape with Los Angeles-type music, a Hollywood film, or movies with porn scenes you wanted, you had to go to Tupkhaneh Square or visit the entrances to the cinemas; cocaine, grass, pills, and ecstasy were to be found in the parks and by the major cross-roads; foreign currency was sold on Ferdowsi Avenue; and ladies from twelve to seventy could be had by the side of all the roads in the city. Trying to make these purchases in the bazaar meant putting up with God only knew what confusion and crowds.

He had not been on speaking terms with Mashallah for several years, and now he was going to ask him for something. He thought some things were too insignificant to bother more important people with; so he was off to see this paragon of a big-hearted man, whose vocabulary didn't contain the word 'no.'

They had known each other for fifteen years, having gotten acquainted while working on a revolutionary committee. In those days, dissident group hideouts were being uncovered faster than they could count. Mashallah would grab the Mojahed kids and the little Communists by the ears and bang their heads against the wall, but when his blood was really on the boil he would pound their heads so hard the plaster would chip and either their ears would come off or their heads would shatter.

Fattah passed the Mahdiyeh and Amin al-Molk sections and, before reaching the sub-bazaar of Hajeb al-Dowleh, he found himself in a market where each shop sold something different: bolts of fabric that shone super-bright and repulsive under the colored fluorescent lights, plastic containers, bits of crystal with air bubbles trapped in them, and large tins displaying every kind of spice and greens for cooking or treating the sick. White ziziphus lotus, henna, indigo, ginger, saffron, and barberries . . . plastic slip-on sandals, toilet articles, cotton fabric for prayer chadors, fabric for blankets, rough muslin for shrouds, men's roomy-crotch pantaloons, white tulle for bridal outfits . . . nickel silver and porcelain, braziers for burning wild rue, crystal water-pipe bowls, plastic tubs for soaking rice and electric pilau cookers, fans made from reeds and gas-operated coolers . . .

Before coming to the Zeyd Bazaar, he reached the carpet market, and, after passing several shop doors, hesitated for a few seconds before finally entering that part of the bazaar. Stacks of rugs rose from the courtyard of the covered serai. Beneath them, in the basement, were the storerooms, while the rug-sellers' offices were ranged around the second-floor balcony. There were a few shops under the stairs where they repaired carpets or sold wool. Fattah asked the serai-keeper about Mashallah and then climbed the uneven, plaster steps to get to one corner of the balcony. Two grey finches eating millet from a crystal bowl were in a cage packed with amulets to ward off the evil eye, and with talismans to keep tongues from wagging.

On the second-floor portico there was also a stock of carpets, from twelve- and nine-meter ones to little one-meter rugs stacked on large wooden and metal pallets. Here and there customers were pawing the carpets with trained hands, counting the knots, and haggling over prices with Mashallah's helpers, who had big paunches and little feet.

The broad portico led to a narrow wooden balcony, at the end of which was Mashallah's shop. The planks of the balcony suddenly began to shake. His whole face from his cheeks to just below his eyes was covered in grey stubble; Mashallah looked up and over his glasses, which were perched on the end of his nose, and saw a heavyset man coming toward him. Squinting, he realized it was Fattah. He rose and the two men hugged.

Mashallah was visibly excited; he called for tea and got out a dish of baklava from a drawer in his desk and placed it before Fattah. He took his prayer beads from his pocket and said, 'Well, well, look who's here! What made you think of me all of a sudden?'

All the while he was nodding, sighing the familiar sighs, and working his beads with the pudgy fingers of his fleshy hand.

Fattah broke off a piece of baklava with his fingers and put it in his mouth. Then he said, 'Your devoted servant.'

Fattah continued to breathe hard, his nostrils quivering with each exhalation. Mashallah pondered him for a moment, then nodded, and once again worked his prayer beads with pudgy fingers.

The sound of people talking came from the courtyard below. Fattah got up and closed the door.

In a way that perhaps signified the time for serious conversation had come, Mashallah, annoyed, said, 'I don't see much of you!'

'Still here, hanging around,' said Fattah.

The two men sat opposite each other at a junky type of desk found in every shop, with lockable draws that opened with a jarring sound, in which were kept large, shabby registers. The registers would open with the help of a saliva-moistened thumb, and the idle hands of their owner would record in them the high figures written by men of little literacy. But now Mashallah's register was on the desk, and there was a pencil sharpened at both ends next to it.

The wall was covered with several small Persian carpets, but, where it was bare, the plaster was flaking or there were bulges. The light on the ceiling had no glass fixture, and the web of wires that led to it was not quite fully covered in fly specks, showing that at one time it had been white. There was a water glass on the desk smudged with fingerprints, and a kerosene stove with a broken mica window and oil stains stood, unlit, at the base of the wall. On the stove was a dirty kettle fitted with a length of wire instead of a proper handle. A large safe and a five-foot refrigerator stood on one side of the room. Fattah sat on one of two broken-down chairs, which creaked every time he shifted his weight.

Mashallah broke the silence. 'Well, you were very busy back in those days, but now . . .!'

Fattah nodded his head in agreement, and, sighing audibly, looked up and said, 'The counter-revolutionaries just wouldn't stop; you too had your hands full! If we hadn't acted . . .'

Then he looked around and said, 'You seem to be sitting pretty.'

He glanced around once more and, with a malicious grin, pointed to the small carpet behind Mashallah. Its edges were suffering from dry rot and, despite the intense reds in the pattern, it had a rainbow of colors that would seemingly shoot sparks with the slightest movement. He said, 'That one must have been excavated, huh?'

Of course Mashallah said nothing, but merely frowned, showing he wasn't in the mood for jokes.

Fattah changed the subject. 'Nowadays you're mostly here, right?'

Mashallah shook his head, 'No way! I go there a couple of days a week.'

'Only a couple of days?' asked Fattah.

Mashallah looked down at the prayer beads in his hand and said, 'They don't let me in on the game much.'

He raised his head again. 'The last time was when we were together.'

A year had passed since their last mission together. They had gone to Urumiyeh to solve a problem with two Christian priests. They decapitated them and put their heads on their chests.

Fattah spread his hands on the table and said, 'I heard that Hajji asked the boys about you, saying you were one of his devoted people. You ought to go and see what's bothering him.'

When Fattah's breath reached Mashallah's face, he recoiled. 'I wrote him at that time and told him that so long as blood flowed through my veins, I was at his service. But these friends of ours are not letting us work.'

'It'll be fine, Mashallah, God willing,' said Fattah.

Both reached for their tea, and, when it seemed there was no more to talk about, Fattah said, 'There is one other matter: Hajji!'

All at once things got serious—perhaps it was Fattah's tone. Mashallah stared at him expectantly. Fattah put another sugar cube under his tongue and filled his mouth with words.

He stopped. Mashallah was still waiting for him to finish the sentence. He put his hands on the desk and leaned forward.

Fattah looked at him for a moment, then said, 'I want to track her down.'

Relaxed, Mashallah said, 'All of them are long gone.'

Fattah pulled back again, leaned in his chair, and said, 'No, this one's still here.'

Mashallah asked, 'So why come to me?'

'I don't want Seyyed to know,' Fattah explained.

'Did you bring it up with your boss?'

'It's not that important,' said Fattah.

'You know I'm on the sidelines out of choice.'

Fattah said, 'I know that, but I also know that the boys in the Section can't say no to you.'

They both remained silent. Mashallah, his eyebrows raised and his lids drooping, looked at the desk; there was no sound except for the click-click of his beads until he said, 'So which singer is it?'

Fattah stroked the desk and said, 'That one . . . the woman, Googoosh.'

Suddenly his mouth began to water, and he looked at his friend. Mashallah opened his mouth to say something, but stayed silent. A kind of heartbreak and longing had crept into Fattah's expression.

Finally Mashallah shuddered and said, 'I just heard that the poor woman has gone out and found herself a husband. She's got worries of her own. Why latch onto her all of a sudden?'

Fattah said, 'I don't want her for myself, Hajji Mashallah! It's just that . . .'

Fattah stopped talking. Smirking, Mashallah looked at him. Fattah slapped his face with his fingertips. 'I'll be damned if I'm lying, Hajji!'

Mashallah said mischievously, 'So . . .?'

Fattah said, 'It's for one of our own boys.'

Smirking, Mashallah wrote a telephone number on a slip of paper and gave it to Fattah. 'I'll be up there the day after tomorrow. Give me a ring the night before to remind me.'

Fattah put the paper in his pocket and, before getting up, tore off a large piece of baklava and put it in his mouth. Then, his mouth full, he said, 'Why don't we get together some time?'

Mashallah said, 'Okay, stay longer. I'll tell the chelow-kabob place to bring us takeout.'

Bringing both hands to his ears, Fattah gestured goodbye and left the shop.

He felt a chill as he emerged from the sub-bazaar, and buttoned his coat. Going behind the shrine, he passed the tailors' alley and the Jews' alley and reached the Zeyd Bazaar, which was the cloth merchants' hall. Bolts of fabric were stacked to the middle of the passageway—most of them somber in color, but they stocked any kind customers wanted.

Carpets were still on his mind. Mashallah had done all right for himself! In that little sliver of a shop he had seen there must have been millions in capital. Then there were the properties he had in Kalar Dasht, the apartment towers he had built with Hashemi in various parts of the city, likewise a couple of factories around Qazvin. But as for himself, he wasn't doing all that badly, either. Hadn't he done his bit sacrificing for the Revolution, relatively speaking? He said to himself, 'The country is in the hands of Muslims, and thank God for it!' He nodded and, suspecting that he may not have been sufficiently grateful, he thanked God again, this time with all his heart.

There was the apartment in Tehran Pars where his mother lived, his own apartment in Elahiyeh; plus, there was the large villa in Nowshahr and the mansion on Kish island, both of which were his, and the couple of factories in which he was a minor shareholder. He put his pocket change in currency-trading and gold; the clinic, with a monthly income approaching four or five million, was a recent offshoot of all these ventures. But what had actually become of the soul that he had laid at the foot of the Revolution?

The Grand Bazaar was like a white-elephant sale of everything from blankets and towels to wallets and the bare torsos of manikins, plastic flowers and ladies' hats, even umbrellas and rope, Indian incense, Calcutta tea and garden fertilizer; likewise prayer CDs, sacks made of hemp and picture postcards of the Eiffel Tower, models of the Holy Ka'ba and the city of Venice. A smoky sordidness rippled visibly on the air.

Fattah went on to the large crossroads, and under the dome turned toward the Friday Mosque Bazaar. Taking the Nowruz Khan steps, he entered Buzergmehri.

He pulled the slip of paper from his pocket and looked at it. He held it in his hand for a moment, and then suddenly crumpled it and looked doubtfully at his fist until he saw her again. The woman had emerged amid a blue haze, with the hat perched at an angle on her head, her round ass wagging, and her eyebrows dancing above those black, devil eyes. He put the crumpled paper in his pocket.

6

Whatever he did, Fattah couldn't get to sleep. He kept tossing and turning and glancing at the part of the window where the curtain was pulled back to reveal the sky. Morning would not come; he had even taken a few hits of vodka, but it had no effect at all except to make him dizzy.

The girl appeared momentarily; then she was gone. She looked at him and a bluish vapor escaped from her lips. She wasn't a girl, she was a salve for the heart with those black eyes, which he saw in the rearview mirror, especially when the car hit a bump; then she frowned in pain and bit her lower lip. It was as if all the blood in her veins rushed to her cheeks.

On this late night in autumn, after all those years of putting girls on beds and sewing up their cuts and tears, now, with his hands plunged between this one's thighs, he felt regret and shame, which were novel feelings. All these years—this was his work, spreading girls' legs on that narrow bed, pushing apart their labia with two fingers, making the thin membranes come together and sewing up their absent virginity; but he had never been tormented by them. Tonight he didn't even go to Sahar's apartment. He didn't feel like it; instead, there were these disturbing thoughts and visions. He got up again and again and smoked a cigarette in the darkness, staring into the corners of the room. All he could see was the girl with that modesty and innocence—each time their glances met, she would lower her head, close her eyes, and recede from him along the wall. It was as though she were reproaching Fattah for what he had done to her.

He hadn't really gone to find Mashallah. Suppose the one he was trying to find was not Googoosh, and suppose those long years of yearning had been only so they could lead to the time when he was nearly forty, and could possess the one person who was so like her or, rather, so like she was in her youth?

All those years, it was true, there were many girls and women; but not one was able to torment him with a look, a sigh, a bashful smile like that. As the days passed, the torment only increased.

Then he recalled a similar feeling, a memory from the distant past that no doubt he remembered because, for months on end, it had prompted that feeling of helplessness in him—just once before, and now twice, after all these years.

He was in high school, and she was the daughter of a neighbor. She was studying on the roof, sitting on the stone stoop with her back against the mud wall of the stairway, when her chador fell to her shoulders. As she reached for it, her black, silky hair with its deep folds glinted. She was smiling, revealing a row of sparkling teeth between two pink lips. Her white legs were moving idly, making her plastic slip-ons rotate. The fifteen-year-old boy had trouble swallowing; his breath caught in his chest, and his heart beat furiously. He was looking down at her from the porch.

The girl would occasionally look up from the book, and, absentmindedly, with a faint smile, her head raised, run her hand through her hair; then she would look back down at the book. Flashes of light seemed to remain in the air for a few seconds. Butterflies flew toward her, and she closed her eyes, raised her head, and faced the sunlight. A butterfly landed on her eyelid; a moment later, having quenched its thirst from her nectar-infused skin, it spread its wings and flew toward the sun.

Spring was drawing to a close, and the trees were laden with cherries. The girl reached out from the roof, grabbed a leaf, and pulled a branch toward her. The leaf tore off and the branch sprang back, sending a cloud of dust into the air; the girl sneezed, perfuming the air with orange blossoms and the dew on the breeze.

Fattah went from the porch to the roof. He stepped over the low wall separating the two homes. He had a long stick in his hand. The girl got up when she saw him disturbing the air and, once again, there was the fragrance of orange and dew.

Fattah snagged the cherry-tree branch with the stick and pulled it toward him. While the branch lay on the mud roof, the girl hurriedly plucked the cherries and put them in a fold in her chador. Fattah let the branch go. A woman came to the window, and from the darkness of the room called out, 'Mahrokh! Mahrokh!'

Mahrokh bit her lip and looked over the roof. The woman at the window said, 'What was that noise?'

'Nothing,' Mahrokh said. 'Just the cat.'

Then the two of them sat with their backs to the stairway wall. Fattah leaned on a row of bricks. Mahrokh pushed his hair back from his forehead and smiled. She picked up cherries one after another, plucked their stems, and put them between her lips, playfully keeping them there, and then sucked them into her mouth and chewed them. Cherry juice gushed out from between her lips, and, as her jaws moved, trickled to the sides of her mouth. With rapture in her eyes she swallowed the cherries, and her throat, which was covered with a fine, blue down, swelled temporarily, then narrowed. Those red lips! Her eyelids lifted, and, sated with the honey of the cherries, her eyes flashed, and fortune like an unfamiliar feeling rippled through the restless heart of the boy. She reached out again and took the next cherry. Fattah stared at her with his mouth half open; then he blinked suddenly and started panting, as if there were little air.

All of a sudden the door to the compound slammed shut. Mahrokh jumped up. She held up her hand as a warning sign. Then there was the sound of shoes shuffling on the brick walk. Mahrokh said, 'God help me! It's my older brother!'

She was afraid. The faint outline of her breasts showed against the thin fabric of her shirt, and her pores exuded a strange odor. Then she put her hands on Fattah's shoulders, 'Run. Run back home. Make sure nobody sees you!'

Those fiery fingers! It was as if the intoxication brought on by an aged wine was coursing through his veins. He touched his shoulder; a nebulous feeling was again running under his skin.

It was like a dream. He didn't see her anymore. The next day he looked and looked from his porch, but the girl didn't come onto the roof— not the next day or the days after. The door to the stairway remained closed, but Fattah was always trying to peek into the compound.

His mother said, 'Fattah, you're imagining things; the house has been empty for quite a while now!'

Fattah went to the roof, then he walked to the edge. There was no sign of a cherry tree, and, bending down, he saw that the compound didn't even have a garden!

The stairway door flapped in the wind, making a scraping noise. Scared stiff, Fattah went through the door and down the stairs, and then found himself in a hallway with several closed doors. There was dust everywhere. He opened one of the doors to find a table, a chair, a carpet, a mirror in a niche, and a lamp. Behind the other door lay a futon, some bed sheets, and embroidered pillows. The satin blankets were moth-eaten in many places, and everything was covered in a layer of dust and had lost its sheen; but it was clear that they had never been used. It was a bridal chamber; its netting had faded, and its wide white ribbons, which had curled and were hanging in places from the wall, had now mostly yellowed.

His mother said they had taken the groom away just before their first time together and he never returned; they got rid of him.

Fattah remembered that the same thing had happened several years before. They grabbed a groom from his house just before the couple's first night together; that time it was the poet that Fattah had shot personally. In those days it wasn't yet customary to hand the job of delivering the coup de grâce over to the 'Repentants,' political prisoners who had turned and 'confessed' their crimes, relieving Fattah of the task.

His eyes burned; he was heartbroken about all those grooms they had taken from their engagement parties or before the first night. But why now, why at this particular moment did his heart break? He wiped his tears with the back of his hand. How long had it been since he last cried? Wasn't he better off in those days? With the Revolution, he started to help out in an operating room. Before that, of course, he was a delivery boy for a liquor store. He strapped customers' orders to the back of his motorcycle and delivered them door to door. Sometimes he got an enormous tip; it didn't involve all that much work. But later on Hasan Khanom got him a place in a hospital where he so scrupulously scrubbed the floors and walls that they sparkled, and he put so much into cleaning that after several months he was made an operating-room aid.

Fattah showed his mettle there as well; of course it didn't involve much work, again, except for getting scissors, clamps, and retractors ready for the autoclave, removing the contaminated cotton from the trays, and applying a special disinfectant to the patient's bed and the operating tables. In his free time he visited the other wards and emptied so much of the patients' waste, urine and feces, cleaned so much of their sputum and phlegm, that the nurses came to rely on him. They taught him how to do injections; they showed him at what angle and at what rate he should inject, and how to ease in the end of the syringe so that it wouldn't hurt, wouldn't cause an abscess, wouldn't nick a muscle. They instructed him on how to draw a blood sample, how to take a patient's temperature, and where and in what order to record what he found on their charts. They taught him all of these things so that when they were busy, he could stand in for them. It didn't take him long to become an old hand; he gave injections without the patient knowing. 'Did you do it?' they'd ask. Fattah would say it was done, and they would ask, 'Then how come I didn't know it?'

They knew him everywhere: in the lab, in radiology, and in the pharmacy, where he learned the names of medicines; in radiology he learned how to put film in the frame, how to center it, and when and how much to push the button; in the vast hospital he was a help to everyone. He'd ingratiated himself with them all; the nurses called him 'Doctor,' and then burst out laughing. If a nurse had a party to go to, or a problem, or was sick, Fattah took over her shift, and all the patients spent that night in peace and comfort; Fattah would provide them with all the tranquilizers they wanted.

In the opening days of the Revolution, when they were bringing in gunshot victims by the truckload, it was clear to everyone that the hospital couldn't operate on all cylinders without him.

After the Revolution was victorious, Hasan Khanom asked him, 'Why are you busting your ass like that? How long do you want to go on washing blood and filth in the operating room?'

Fattah asked, 'What should I do?' Hasan Aqa took him by the hand to a revolutionary committee set up near the neighborhood. He was to become, if fate allowed, one fine day, the capital's most skillful surgeon.

At the committee they asked him whether he could drive and whether he had a license. Fattah didn't have a license, but said he did. Then they presented him to the administration, and he became the driver for one of the brothers they called Brother Mohsen. In the morning he would pick up Brother Mohsen and two others and take them here and there. One of them was an expert in antiques, the other knew about paintings. Fattah brought them to the Shah's palaces or those of his relatives, to the palatial homes of the elite, to basements full of crystal, silver, and objects from the ancient past. The antiques expert, the one they called 'Doctor,' had a flashlight and a monocle. He picked up the antiques, positioned them this way and that, turned them, held them up to the light, and nodded his head. At times he would stop and say, 'This is not something for me; for an accurate assessment you need to call in Professor I-don't-know-who,' and Brother Mohsen would note everything. If it were a small thing, naturally he would pick it up and put it in his pocket.

The other brother was called Fokuri. One time they went to a place where there was a painting of several half-naked women on the wall. Brother Mohsen kept repeating, 'Forgive me, Lord.' He wouldn't look directly at the picture; rather he glanced at it from an angle and ordered that they take it down immediately to see what they wanted to do with it.

Mr. Fokuri tugged at his goatee and asked in a measured voice, 'Do you know the price of this painting?'

Brother Mohsen said, 'In my opinion, both should be burned.'

Mr. Fokuri said, 'This is Golden Age stuff, a masterpiece of André Derain!'

'Look at what the back-stabbing Zionists have painted!' said Brother Mohsen.

Fokuri said, 'For the human form there's never been a better painter than Derain. Look at how those women have been painted! The master sure knew where to put his brush.'

Brother Mohsen said, 'Just look at how early the Zionists began to do their work!'

Then they reached a marble statue of a young naked girl lying down, holding a bunch of grapes over her mouth. The girl's breasts had newly sprouted and, naturally, were small enough to fit in one's fist. Brother Mohsen blinked twice. Apparently he wasn't sure he was awake. Now panting in earnest, he said, 'No doubt this one we've got to destroy.'

Then he went to the edge of the garden to find a stone. Mr. Fokuri began to beg. Brother Mohsen had turned his face to the wall.

Mr. Fokuri said, 'This statue has fans in every corner of the world.'

Brother Mohsen said, 'They can all drop dead as far as I'm concerned, the statue and its fans!'

After a couple of years, they sent Fattah to Evin. They had just expelled Bani Sadr, and the counter-revolutionary movement was mobilized to strike at the Revolution. Fattah would deliver the coup de grâce and then would hose down the area and remove clumps of gore. An hour later, after the water had dried, they put the corpses in the back of a pickup and brought them to Khavaran Road to dump them in a ditch. At times when Fattah was loading the bodies into the truck, they were still warm, or their hands would move, or their eyelids would flutter. Once when a swollen breast popped out from a soaked shirt clinging to a body, Fattah looked around warily and put the nipple in his mouth.

There was no more room in the cells, which meant every hallway was full of traitors sitting blindfold, waiting to be interrogated—all perfectly innocent, it seemed. The place was filled with hustle and bustle, cries and screaming, spattered with blood, vomit, and urine. Loudspeakers were forever blaring prayers, sermons, and military marches.

So busy he didn't have time to scratch his head, Fattah could be kept there all night. He was gradually losing his wits because of the pressure of the work; that was why he asked to be sent back to the committee for another assignment. The members would point out a home, which a group would swoop down on, confiscate the video player, then drag the homeowner before the committee. After all, they couldn't just sit twiddling their thumbs, watching while people were doing indecent things, could they?

Weddings and celebrations where men and women mixed! Another attack: women heavily made up and not a hair out of place, tattooed eyebrows and nose jobs, tried to hide behind one another and covered their heads with anything that came to hand. Fattah remembered that once a woman emptied a fruit basket and put it upside down on her head. They gathered the men in one corner and said, 'You call yourselves self-respecting! Would a real man let his good name be trampled in the mud like that?'

The men would look away and sheepishly explain, 'We're no match for them; can't you forgive them just this one time?' Then they would shout at the men, load the women in trucks and take them away.

Nights they would spend at the crossroads and stop cars with G3s in their hands. First they'd ask for licenses, then they'd inspect the trunks, and last they'd look the passengers up and down. These were moments of suspense and waiting; the women would bring the hems of their skirts over their knees and push their hair back under their headscarves and hunch over, becoming smaller and smaller—each trying to hide behind the other. The committee men would frown and issue clipped, emphatic commands: this car go, that one stay, bring this man, take that woman. Of course, they would note the locks of hair that had escaped from the scarves, the nail polish on a hand that had emerged from a pocket without meaning to; then they'd order everybody out of the car. When it was the men's turn, they told them to say 'Haaa,' and they did. Fattah would suddenly sit back and make a face; the stench of alcohol on their breath offended his sense of smell. Denial was no use, and they forced the men to drink boiling water until they threw up. They would send a sample to the laboratory, which would confirm the presence of alcohol. The guilty would be whipped.

When Fattah looked back, he saw that his life was taken out of the pages of history; first he arrested SAVAK agents and the corrupt who prospered under the Shah, then it was the turn of the Demokrats, the hypocrite Mojahedin, Communists, and infidels, then the coup-plotters and the American spies, and finally the economic terrorists. The exorcism machine was working overtime, and they got all the devils and took them away until the nation was on its way to becoming a paradise on earth, pure and cleansed. But all of a sudden up popped the Mullah-begotten and people who grow fat on the economic favors of the government, acting as if there were no tomorrow, with men in power behind them.

That morning he got out of bed feeling down, a bitter taste in his mouth; he washed his face and hands, got dressed and, without having so much as a cup of unsweetened tea, left the house. His eyes went blank for a second. He drove and stopped at the end of their alley, waiting in the car and staring at their front door. No one came out, and he kept looking at his watch. Finally the door opened and Shahrzad emerged, and then closed the door behind her. Fattah started the car and drove. He passed the girl and came to a stop ahead of her; he honked, bent down and opened the window and said, 'Get in!'

Fattah said this in such a friendly way that Shahrzad was not startled. But she did look around and say, 'Hello, Doctor. You . . . here?'

Fattah nodded and, with a tired look, said calmly and sadly, 'Get in!'

This time he said it so poetically that Shahrzad had to laugh; she looked at his gloomy, sleep-deprived face and, perhaps feeling sorry for him, said, 'I don't want to be a bother, Doctor.'

Fattah said again, 'I said: get in!'

This time Shahrzad was startled by his tone, which hinted at coercion. She said, 'I'm not going far, I'm going . . . going around here only a few . . .'

Patiently, Fattah said, 'No problem; I'll drive you.'

At once he was again infinitely sad. Shahrzad said, 'I'm not going far, I said!'

Fattah turned, and, with a loud exhalation and a harsh and humorless voice announced, 'I said, I'll drive you.'

Shahrzad looked at the sidewalk indecisively and felt help-less, but didn't want to show it. Then she grabbed the handle of the back door. Fattah said, 'In front!'

Shahrzad hesitated, her hand still on the back door handle and her eyes on the sidewalk. Fattah turned his head around completely, trying to catch her glance. Shahrzad didn't move, but after a moment raised her head and directed that look, which was never fixed, always searching about, at him. What did Fattah see in that look that finally made him turn back, stare straight ahead, and, in the same muted tone say, 'Fine, have it your way'?

Shahrzad opened the door and sat down. She felt uneasy; a wave of fear traveled upward from her toes.

Fattah started driving. Shahrzad straightened the chador on her head. Looking at her in the mirror, Fattah said, 'I want to talk to you for a bit.'

Shahrzad immediately let go of the side flaps of her chador, which had been on her shoulders, leaned forward and asked, 'Now?'

This time, the quiver of fear found its way to her heart. Fattah turned toward her.

'What's wrong with now?'

'What about?'

'Now, I'm saying!' said Fattah.

Then he nodded, asking her to be calm, despite the obvious insecurity that filled the closed atmosphere of the car like smoke.

Shahrzad leaned back. 'I was about to go to class.'

It was hard to hear her voice; Fattah asked, 'Class?'

Shahrzad looked out the window, and, now suddenly indifferent, said, 'I go to sewing classes.'

Fattah's face lit up. 'So, take today off! How 'bout it?'

Shahrzad froze. After a moment, she said, 'What if my mother finds out?'

Imitating her, Fattah said, '*What if my mother finds out?*'

He wasn't in a joking mood, either, and said soberly, 'Fine. Those other times, how did you manage to slip out of the house without your mother knowing?'

They looked at each other in the mirror for a time. Shahrzad's eyes filled with tears.

Embarrassed, Fattah shook his hand in the air and said, 'Hand on the Qur'an, I don't mean to hurt you!'

Then he looked outside. He pounded the steering wheel with his fist and said, 'I just want you to be with me!'

Shahrzad again let go of the chador flaps under her chin. She moved her lips and leaned forward a little, then she swallowed audibly, suddenly covered her face with the chador, and started to bawl.

Embarrassed again, Fattah looked around, said a *Forgive me, Lord* and shook his head with a mixture of helplessness and rage. As if it were the only thing he could do, he pressed down on the gas pedal harder and harder. Then, with that whiny voice used by the helpless on the verge of tears, he said, 'I swear to God, I'm not going to harass you.'

Was it possible to be unkind to her? It was impossible for anyone caught in those two fetching, caring eyes, especially when they were sorrowful or teary, to stay calm.

By now they had reached streets with names that Shahrzad didn't know, but she kept on crying anyway. Fed up, Fattah said, 'I'll just come and ask for your hand, okay? I accept all your conditions. Is that fine with you? Please don't cry anymore, I'm begging you; people are staring.'

Shahrzad uncovered her face; her eyelashes were almost stuck together—she was wailing like a baby with a face full of tears. Fattah said, 'Don't wail like that, girl, you're killing me!'

He wasn't lying, but was saying it as if it were he who was choked up.

Between sobs, Shahrzad said, 'I told you that in a couple of weeks they're coming to arrange the preliminaries for my marriage!'

Fattah jammed on the brakes needlessly. As he stared at Shahrzad in the rearview mirror, he leaned his chest against the steering wheel. Then he pulled himself back, breathed heavily while he gazed out his window, and in a voice that seemed to be directed inward, said, 'The preliminaries will never happen; you belong to me!'

He said it forcefully in a tone that brooked no contradiction; he even convinced himself that his was the final decision. Then he gave a confirming nod, and was off again.

Shahrzad had stopped crying; her eyes were wide open as she stared, terrified, at the back of the man's neck. Then, with a sudden decisiveness, she raised her voice and growled, 'Stop!'

Without thinking, he put his foot on the brake. Shahrzad flew out of the car like a sparrow.

7

Fakhri had just put on her prayer shawl when she heard the front door close; she knew it was Fattah. He had a key; she wondered how long had it been since he last visited her. Groaning, Fakhri went into the bending-forward position of her prayer and heard the sound of Fattah in the hall.

'Where are you, dear? Where, darling?'

In a loud voice, she said a *God is great*, and rose from bending; then, still groaning, struggled with her full prostration. Fattah entered the room and sat on the chair behind the door, waiting for her to finish. The woman seemed crumpled from behind. In the old days few women could move the way she did, but now the slightest movement would make her joints ache so she'd wish she were dead. The old days, those days the sisters dubbed her 'Mother Fakhri' and idolized her—where had they gone? *How* had they gone? When she stood in front of the University of Tehran, singlehandedly cordoning off the length of the street, you wouldn't hear a peep out of the fledgling Mojahedin and Communists. What was left of that woman now?

As Fakhri put her hand before her to say the special prayer, she calculated that it had been eighteen days since Fattah had come to see her: mothers sacrifice their souls for their children—see what happens when they grow up! Especially in her case, being both mother and father for the child. The only thing his bastard father had been good for was to get her knocked up, bid farewell, and leave. Fakhri immediately went into action and, like a cat, snatched the baby from the tramps, drunks, and street singers on Lalehzar Avenue and made something of him.

After completing the first part of the prayer, she tried to raise herself on those swollen legs. Fakhri let out such groans it made Fattah very sad. In her white prayer shawl, and on that deep-red prayer mat, the woman seemed to him the purest being on earth, something he had only recently realized. From the time of his stepfather Hasan Khanom's death, this woman had been alone. In the last few years, she had become feeble, meaning she was even more alone.

All of a sudden Fattah wanted to do his ablutions and say his prayers. This was a recent need, a sudden urge; no such feelings had ever visited him before.

Fakhri lifted her head from the mat, 'May the light rain down on your grave, Hasan Khanom! This man became a father to my orphan child; he brought us out of that damned place and made it good for us in the end.'

Fattah was no more than six when Hasan Khanom lifted him from the floor, put him on his lap, and said, 'Look, this child's going to die here.' Hasan took Fakhri on a pilgrimage, absolved her of her sins, and married her.

Fakhri finished her prayers and was wiping the moisture from her eyes with the back of her hand when Fattah kissed her head from behind.

Fakhri turned around and said reproachfully, 'What a surprise!'

Fattah returned to his seat, sat down, and said, 'May they be answered, Mama!'

Fakhri sighed and looked at her son.

Fattah blurted out, 'I have a sweetheart, Mama!'

There wasn't a hint of sarcasm in his tone, which startled Fakhri. Then with his eyes on his mother he nodded slowly.

Fakhri reached out for the tie of her wimple and turned it around, freeing her head; then she turned her back on her son and wrapped it up in her prayer mat.

There was no harm in falling for someone; after all, hadn't it happened to Fakhri herself when she was just a little kid?

Fakhri said, 'What's eating you, darling?'

Fattah said immediately, 'I'm scared . . . scared that they won't give the girl to me!'

Fakhri turned, put her hands on her hips, and with a wrinkled brow, said, 'Who does she think she is, the daughter of the big cheese up north?'

Fattah put his hand up and said, 'No, it's absolutely nothing like that!'

Fakhri said, 'So, what is it then? . . . What do they say? Tell me.'

'Nothing, yet,' Fattah said. 'She has no father, and I haven't spoken to the mother yet.'

Fakhri swiveled her head, apparently thinking, and said, 'A girl with no father! That's some girl!'

Fattah erupted, 'She's not one of them!'

Fakhri raised her voice, 'Well, that's what they all say when you ask them.'

85

Fattah swatted the air, impatient. 'We've got to wait and see if they actually give her to me.'

Fakhri said bitterly, 'Why shouldn't they?'

Fattah placed one hand on the other and said, 'Her age . . . she's young!'

'How old?' asked Fakhri contentiously.

Fattah pursed his lips. 'Something like eighteen, nineteen.'

Fakhri bent forward, made a wry face and, with her head tilted, said, 'Do you know how old I was when I gave birth to you? Fourteen, going on fifteen!'

They used to live in Amin al-Soltan Square; there was a teahouse at the head of their alley. That was the low point in her life, the point from which she was propelled, without warning, into the midst of life's great show.

People sat in Amin al-Soltan Square, at a teahouse at the beginning of their alley, a pleasant spot with water gurgling in the channel beside the road and chirping canaries in cages. There was a breeze, too, blowing from the fields of Varamin, bringing with it the fragrance of soil and vegetables. Coming to the reed mats covering the wooden platform, which were spotted with sprinkled water, filled a person with a kind of glee, moving him to sing, and, if there were any grounds for it, fall in love.

Most of the teahouse customers were truck drivers bringing squash, cucumbers, and eggplants from Varamin to Tehran. After they unloaded their trucks, they would sit on the carpet-covered platforms in the shade of the plane trees by the channel and drink tea from glasses with sugar cubes beside them.

The teahouse also had a radio that played popular songs. The owner, Mashdi, mostly lounged about, while his apprentice, Abdollah, ran the shop. Mashdi would pack the bowls of the water pipes with tobacco at the rear of the place, or fill the samovar burners with charcoal; after completing these tasks, he'd fiddle with the knobs on the radio. When his back gave him trouble, he'd sometimes take a small snuff box of opium from his sash, open the lid, and pop a piece the size of a mouse dropping into his mouth.

One of the customers was a burly young man with a handlebar mustache, a chest full of wooly hair, and scars from knife wounds in a couple of places on his face. Whenever a song by Abdolvahab ended, and the radio started preaching about the use of quinine, he would explode, 'Turn that crap off, will you, Mashdi!'

Mashdi would do so in the blink of an eye; then he would break into song himself. And it was as if a hand had reached into Fakhri's body and tugged at her heartstrings, and she would run to the beginning of the alley.

One day, Fakhri had gone to the grocer's next to the teahouse to buy some whey, oil, or jujubes, and the young man saw her and winked. Fakhri couldn't help but smile too and, holding her chador tight over her face, rushed to her doorstep. Then she went back and looked toward the beginning of the alley; the young man was standing with his legs apart, hands on hips; looking back at her, he started to snigger. There wasn't much distance between them; Fakhri could even see the flash of the gold crown on his front tooth.

Fakhri would go there every day, and the young man would be sitting there in the same place, or reclining on a wooden platform, looking at her through narrowed eyelids, winking, bringing a smile to Fakhri's lips. One day Fakhri stood in the middle of the alley so long that the young man walked over to her. The next day he took her for a ride in the desert, and, along the way, he bought her a clay jar of mulberries.

It was a chilly summer, and the desert was covered in green; weeds were even growing on the clumps of earth strewn by the wall of an ice cave. He embraced Fakhri, lifted her in the air and put her on his lap; Fakhri took the mulberries out of the jar one by one and put them in her mouth; her hands and lips had become crimson, and the man kept kissing them. She hadn't reached the bottom of the jar when she began to notice the young man's smell, which was like the smell of her father's sleeveless vest that her mother had given to her to wash. Then she felt how good the smell was, both pungent and having a kind of warmth, and how it sent a subtle wave coursing through her veins, a special feeling that she found pleasurable and frightening at the same time.

Fakhri's nostrils quivered, and she was still exploring the new feeling brought on by the male smell when his strange eyes rolled back into his head; at that very moment he had taken her virginity. Finally, when he was standing by a bush peeing, the lump in Fakhri's throat burst and she began to wail—what a wail!

The man said to himself, 'For God's sake!' and shook his head, and, as pee gushed forth, said to her, 'Don't cry; I'll marry you.'

She believed him and quieted down, but time took a sudden turn, distancing itself from her; pieces of the past had yet to link up with the future, and some of the pieces were covered in mist, while others took on an incredible luminosity, and in one of these she saw herself wearing a white wedding dress; on her head were paper flowers and tiny lanterns; then she smiled, her cheeks tear-moistened. The man shook his member and pulled up his trousers; he went to her and kissed her lips. It seemed as if stars shot from her flushed cheeks.

From time to time he would take her out to the desert, and as always put her on his lap; after one or two shakes, his eyes would roll back, and a moment later he'd be contented; each time he bought her something. One day he saw Fakhri vomiting over a ditch. After that, he went about setting the stage for the lousy way he was going to treat her; he would find fault with her over something, and kick her in the side and stomach. The baby did not abort, and Fakhri's belly grew by the day; her face took on a greater innocence; kindness may have even radiated from her hands, and a certain solemnity distanced her from the realm of childhood, all of which made the man angry. His visits to the teahouse became less frequent; he was making himself scarce.

Her father sensed what was going on, but didn't yell and scream, didn't beat her, nothing! He just threw her out of the house. He stood in the yard with his legs apart pointing to the gate and said, 'Go, go find some dump where you can bring your little brat into the world, bury it there, and then, if you want, come back home.'

With tears in her eyes, her mother tied a piece of bread and a set of clothing in a bundle for her. 'Go!' she said.

She wanted to ask where she should go, but didn't; she grabbed the bundle and left the house and went to the head of the alley. She sat on the edge of one of the platforms at the teahouse and stared at the street. Mashdi kept bringing her tea until sundown, telling her constantly that he would show up; but he didn't. The neighborhood kids circled her, flinging stones and taunting her; Mashdi would chase them halfway down the alley and come back to the teahouse short of breath. That night Fakhri, using the bundle as a pillow, lay down and watched the stars until dawn. The next day she waited again, but the man had no intention of coming.

At noon, she picked up the bundle and went on her way. Mashdi followed her, begging her to stay, saying he was bound to turn up. Rubbing her stomach, she walked on, turned into the alley and was gone.

Seeing her, men would lick their chops and say politely, 'Be my guest!' One pointed to the door of his upstairs room, another offered his donkey's saddle blanket, and yet another proposed a ride on the back of his bike. Men sized up every spot on her body with their eyes; one found her eyes and brows the size of his hand; another found her ass nicely rounded and wide; while another . . . Why go on? Suffice to say that before she had reached the next street, fifty people wanted to pick her up—she was certainly young, but meaty. Finally there was one old man—may God forgive his father's sins—who took care of her. Fakhri was cute and full-bodied with a fine voice, and the old man had a café with half-naked dancers on Lalehzar. It was in the basement of that café where she gave birth to Fattah.

During the day she worked in the kitchen, and nights she would sing when the musicians took their break. There was a slightly sorrowful strain in her singing, and the customers who were wild about that doleful undertone wouldn't let her off the stage. She would sing so many encores her voice cracked, and men would be moved to tears. Then she would go among the crowd of drunken men and stop at every table; with their last drinks, the men would drink to the health of Fattaneh—that was the stage name they gave her. Then they would throw their dark jackets over their shoulders, and at dawn, worn and wasted, they would file out of the café one by one. Fakhri's work would begin in earnest after they had left. Wearing a well-worn man's shirt, she would turn the chairs over, put them on the tables, and wash the floor with bucket after bucket of water. After an hour she couldn't stand upright, and like a corpse, soaking wet, she'd go to bed as it was getting light.

At the end of the night Fakhri's satin blouse, with its bright purples, oranges, and dark reds, glowed like a lantern in the dusky light, which was swirling with clouds of smoke; this caused the drunken men, who would arrive home after about an hour, to experience flashes of such colors in their daybreak dreams. She had, of course, a couple of fellow performers, but it was for her that men flocked to the café. The drunken whispers, romantic murmurings, sweet nothings that they all knew were not to be believed, nevertheless enveloped them in a profound but short-lived reverie. Fakhri fondled them, and they would suddenly become quiet little lambs; she would tease them at times, and be serious at others, and, without realizing it, scream at them: 'Go home now, you shits! There are women who've been thrashing about in bed waiting for you so long, they've died!'

True, she was also soft-hearted; one time Fattah came to her, sleepy-eyed, grabbed her skirt with his little fist and asked resentfully, 'Mommy, why don't you come and sleep by me?' She choked up, and no matter how sarcastically she kidded the two drunken men on either side of her, kissing and slobbering up and down her naked arms from the tips of her fingers to her shoulders, the lump in her throat wouldn't go away.

Hasan Khanom, sitting to one side, came over and petted the boy's head, and it wasn't clear whether there were tears on his face because the child was defenseless or because of his own loneliness. He only said, 'It's not fair for this child to go to waste in this sort of place.'

'What can I do?' asked Fakhri. The lump in her throat burst, and she started to cry so hard all conversation stopped.

Hasan Khanom pulled the men away from her arms, and, with a reproachful, rasping voice, said, 'This darling little boy doesn't deserve to grow up in this dump.'

He picked up Fattah and put him on his lap. Again Fattaneh repeated, 'What can I do?' and began to sob.

Hasan Khanom placed himself right where, but for a few of the drunks, there was no one but himself, Fattaneh, and God, and said to her, 'I'll marry you, and I'll get an ID for your child myself.'

Fattaneh had seen him before, sitting quietly, not making any trouble in the crowd; he seemed wrapped up in himself, as if he had known failure in love.

He whisked Fakhri off to the Shah Abdolazim shrine where she sought absolution; then he notified the Mullah, and they were married. He took her to his home in the old quarter of Darkhungah, and it was in his home that Fakhri learned to live a decent life. And it was there too the neighbor women taught her how to do ablutions. Before that, she hadn't even heard of these things; and it was there she found out that there were specific terms for a woman who had her period two months in a row but not on the same day each month, and for a woman whose period was not a fixed number of days; and she learned that after each menstruation she had to clean herself well and then go to the public bath to do her ablutions so she could pray. The same neighbor women taught her the customs if the bath had a heated pool, or if it had a shower, how to work it; this was all difficult for her at first, and she kept making mistakes, but in the end she learned.

At this point, she remembered her mother sometimes packing up her fresh dresses and towels and saying that she had to go to the bath before she could do a two-prostration prayer. Fakhri also started frequenting the plays held for the Passion of the Imam, as well as fasting during Ramadan, except on those days when she had her period. Prior to the evening prayer, she would switch on the radio and before they said the *Our Lord*, a feeling of spirituality would come over her.

Hasan Khanom had an acquaintance in the great Tehran cemetery, and he got Fakhri a job there. The cemetery had a place they washed bodies where everything was automated, something Fakhri had never heard of. There were streets there, fountains, lawns, a reception unit, and even a police station. Everything about it was automated; the names of the dead were entered in a computer, the graves were numbered, and the names of the bodies were on an electronic display in the waiting room even before the deceased was shrouded and buried. They rented out loudspeakers; the professional prayer-readers and declaimers of the Qur'an had fixed rates; and in rooms all the same size, they sold flowers for placing on gravestones. The streets were broad, the gardens full of flowers, and a total of fifty people watered the lawns twenty-four hours a day. There were donation boxes posted everywhere, and all the professional prayer-readers, gravediggers, and beggars wore uniforms. The amount of alms was fixed—there was a fine for any infraction—and for dead people without family or friends, they rented out professional lamenters and expert moaners, whose rates never went up except for inflation. The text of the *Prayer of Fright*, said for the dead on their first day in the grave, was plastered to the wall of the body-washers' building. They said the standard prayer for the dead outside of it in front of the coffin; for the deceased man it was one thing, for a woman it was different. They brought the dead from the body-washers to the burial site in a hearse; there they dug the grave and the stone slab was made ready. The cemetery was like Tehran; it had an uptown and a downtown, with rates that varied depending on one's finances. Uptown was for fortune's favorites, downtown for the damned.

While on trips with her mother to the shrine of Seyyed Malek Khatun, Fakhri had seen them washing bodies a few times. When the wife of a neighbor had died, they washed her body right in the kitchen—that is, her mother washed the body, having pulled back the flaps of her chador and tied them behind her head. A couple of other women stood beside her, pouring water over the corpse while her mother washed the body down with a cloth and soap.

The automated body-washer establishment had lots of rules and regulations. Fakhri had to wear a long smock, an apron, gloves, a mask, and boots; there was a hatch with a short canvas curtain in front of it, through which, on a gurney-like thing that made a noise, they wheeled in the corpses. There they first stripped the bodies and put them on a marble slab. The steps for washing the dead were like those for washing after sex; they washed the hands three times, then the genital region, the heads with foam made from wild jujube trees—also three times—the right side, then the left, and, finally, they patted the whole body with their hands. Washing with jujube powder was only the first round; the two subsequent washings were just the like the first, except one was with camphor water and the other with pure water. The whole time they would say *Seek Forgiveness*, and put the corpse on the niche stone. That was when Fakhri went to work. After applying sweet herbs to the body, she put mignonette on some cotton to plug the genital orifices; then she wound a fine loincloth and plugged their assholes, and the shrouded body was ready to go on to the next stage on the gurney-like thing.

It was at the body-washers' building that she lost her fear of dying. She said to herself that there was nothing more to it: someone suddenly drops dead. It was a cycle: one comes into the world, another goes. It might happen sooner or later, but it would definitely happen! She worked there for a few years until she got fed up, then left. She said to herself, *There is also life out there; it isn't all death!*

With each passing day she moved further away from the past, so that except for a couple of things, nothing remained.

Among those things were movies with Fardin, featuring the offal stews of the local haunts and cafés, and the mosques with their domes and garish Hamsa Hands. These things also belonged to the past, as well as the gramophone and thousands of records that were all Mahvash and Davud Qa'em Maqami songs.

8

Khanjan opened the door a crack; he was sleeping on the floor on a futon, a large pillow under his head. His snores made the roof shake. She called him again, and this time he stopped snoring. Khanjan said, 'It's noon already, and you're not up! It's noon!'

The blanket moved, Mostafa turned over, and a moment later rose suddenly. Khanjan said, 'You'll be late. You told me to wake you at eight!'

His eyes half open, Mostafa shook his head and fell back on the futon saying, 'One day you're gonna let me sleep as long as I want!'

Khanjan hadn't closed the door as she said, 'Get up. I have good news for you!'

Mostafa shot up and sat on the futon, his puffy eyes full of curiosity. Only a pelt of thick hair covered his bare chest; Khanjan frowned, closed the door and said, 'Get dressed!'

Mostafa raced to get his shirt on, folded the futon and went to the hall, where Khanjan was sitting behind her sewing machine, surrounded by scraps of cloth.

'What is it? Tell me!'

He sat down in front of his mother, expecting her to say something. Khanjan glanced at her son out of the corner of her eye and smiled. She made a cute gesture with her head and said, 'They told us to come and talk about it.'

Mostafa howled for joy, put his hands under his mother's arms, and lifted her into the air. Khanjan started to shout and scream. Mostafa spun her around once and then put her back on the ground.

'I heard my bones crack, sweetie!' she grumbled. 'You almost tore me limb from limb!'

'When?' asked Mostafa.

Khanjan patted herself on the shoulders and said, 'I've got to send for your uncle so we can all go together. It's not like we have no family!'

Mostafa went into the courtyard, where Mirza, his grandfather, was sitting on a rock under a grape trellis quietly reading the Qur'an.

Mostafa said hello.

'Up at the crack of dawn today?' asked Mirza sarcastically.

He looked at him for a few moments, smiling and shaking his head. Mostafa paid no attention and went to the bathroom, and Mirza returned to his reading, his upper body rocking rhythmically, like a pendulum. The old man, the rocking, and the grapevine with its emerald droplets capturing the autumn light, resembled a lost land. Something seemed to rise from him and spread through the air, something colorless. It was not earthly, either; maybe it had an element of the human imagination, because it was light and could penetrate everywhere, all at once.

Mostafa emerged from the bathroom huffing and puffing and went to the font. He opened the spigot and said, 'Grandpa, grab your hat and coat; I'm going courting!'

Mirza looked at the boy over his glasses, shook his head sagely, and resumed his reading. Mostafa splashed his face with water and returned to the hall with his head still wet.

Khanjan raised the wick of the samovar and spread the tablecloth on the floor. The water began to bubble, and steam climbed into the air. Her one and only son was to be married. She remembered the Thursday nights when she would take him by the hand and bring him to Jamkaran. Mostafa would throw the drawings he had painted with his little hands into the well, a replica of the place the Twelfth Imam went into hiding. Khanjan cried with all her heart and prayed for the appearance of the Twelfth Imam.

Mostafa declared, 'Tonight I'll go and get Uncle myself!'

There was the sound of people saying, *There is no God but Allah* in the distance; Khanjan muttered, 'It's probably a funeral.'

Then she looked up at the ceiling and murmured a prayer.

'What do you mean, funeral?' said Mostafa. 'It's a wedding, a *wedding!*'

Then, snapping his fingers, he shook his behind. Khanjan took the kettle from the samovar and filled the glasses. Mostafa was still shaking his ass.

Khanjan looked her son up and down for a second and, her mood changing all of a sudden, said, 'Did you see about that girl?'

Mostafa kept on snapping his fingers and waving his behind around. Khanjan glared at her son's round little ass and screeched, 'Well?'

As soon as he heard his mother's screech, Mostafa stopped abruptly, leaving his plump little rear to dry in the wind. 'What happened?' he asked.

Khanjan regarded her son reproachfully and said, 'Didn't I tell you to go and see about that poor girl?'

'Which girl?' Mostafa asked.

Then he suddenly realized his mistake and said, 'Oh, yeah, I found her; I told them nobody has the right to lay a finger on her!'

He said this as if the one he had supposedly told was still in front of him, and he wagged his finger in the air.

Khanjan's mood improved and said, 'Okay, dear, may God reward you! If you only knew how much Ezzat Sadat was begging and pleading!'

Mostafa said, 'You've got nothing to worry about, not a thing!'

Khanjan said, 'You know, my darling, they took the girl by surprise, surrounding her right in the middle of the street, and for no reason at all threw her into a car and took her away.'

Mostafa shook his head in disbelief. Khanjan continued, 'It's not me who's saying this; the shopkeepers in the neighborhood told me!'

Mostafa said, 'First thing tomorrow I'll take personal charge of her so everybody can rest easy!'

Khanjan, satisfied, nodded and got back to work.

Mostafa scratched his ear and said, 'We've got to think about a ring, some earrings, all that stuff, you know?'

Khanjan held her arms apart and said, 'What's the rush? You want to do this now? A box of sweets is enough for the time being!'

Mostafa scratched his ear again and said, 'This time we'll take Grandpa with us, and the next time Uncle, so he can—'

Khanjan raised her head and, interrupting her son, said, 'He's not coming!'

Mostafa knelt before his mother. 'Why?'

Khanjan said, 'He's not happy about this union.'

Mostafa pushed away something in the air and asked, 'How come?'

Khanjan sighed. 'He's read the omens with the Qur'an three times!'

Then she nodded slowly in despair. Mostafa kept his eyes on her. Khanjan said, 'They're not good!'

Mostafa got to his feet and, raising his voice, said, 'You don't have to consult the Qur'an for everything.'

'I wasn't the one who asked him to,' Khanjan said hurriedly.

Mostafa went to the window. Mirza was still reading the Qur'an. Mostafa turned toward his mother and said angrily, 'With all these dos and don'ts of his, he's ruining my life!'

Khanjan made a sour face. 'You're not one to listen, are you?'

Mostafa said, 'Why don't we send him to Uncle's place for a while?'

Khanjan said, 'The house isn't big enough for you, is that it?'

Mostafa said, 'It isn't like we're criminals deserving to be punished, is it?'

Fed up, Khanjan turned away and said, 'I'll never put my poor old father in the care of that wife of your uncle's!'

Mirza's obsession with religion had driven everyone crazy. He'd never touch anything with wet hands; he was careful everywhere. When the television showed women without their hair covered, Mirza would sit with his back to it. Khanjan would say, 'The women are infidels, foreigners; it won't matter if you see their hair.'

He wouldn't listen. He'd shake his head and keep on sitting with his back to the television. The television also played songs and music, which were even worse than bareheaded women.

Mirza wrote sayings on paper to put in amulets. He knew all the collections by heart: *The Grand Compendium* of Ja'far, *The Alexander Talismans, The Veiled Secret,* and *The Trove of al-Hoseyni.* He knew how to do numerology and interpret dreams; he explained the mathematical values of letters, and had down pat the inauspicious days and the rules of divination. He knew, for example, when the crops would be hit by blight; when there would be famine and want; when the peasants would overcome the rulers; and when the meek would avenge themselves on the mighty. He knew when there would be eclipses—solar and lunar—and bread shortages; when camels would get mange; when there would be locusts on the crops and bread would become expensive; and when a comet would appear in the sky, a sure sign of war. Four-circle and six-circle divinations looked like the illustration opposite:

At night, he would lie awake fretting about the abundance of sin and the torments of hell. He would awake around dawn, leave his bed, put on his cloak with his back bent, and go to the edge of the font to do his ablutions with cold water; there he would raise his head for a moment, searching for the moon. Then, when he got back to his room, he would spread

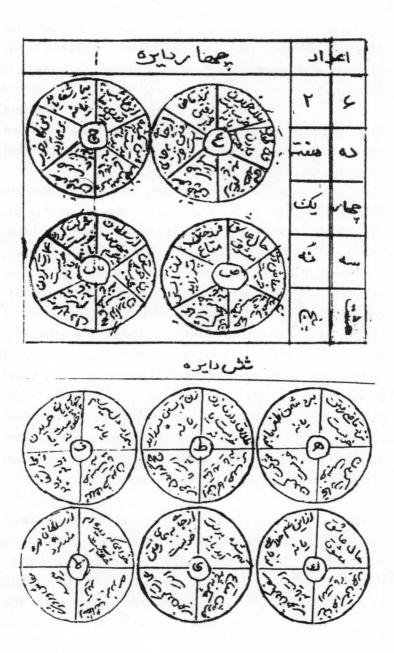

his prayer mat and start the preliminaries. He cried so much while praying that his face would drip with tears. In the morning after the mandatory and volitional prayers it was time for the common post-prayers, and after that, the special prayers. In addition, he had a daily ritual of separate prayers and on Fridays even more involved, devotional activities: there were the Denary Prayers and the Prayers of the Signs; saying the Consultation Prayer was on his daily agenda, twice a day; and recently he had other special benedictions for every waking hour. Such were the ways, month after month, he showed his indifference to worldly goods and his devotion to the Lord.

Mirza had been a carpenter. He shut up shop after the death of his wife. How much longer did he have to live, after all? Mirza believed worldly goods blinded a man. All he had in his kitchen were a table spread for food and a pitcher for water. He fasted most days. After his evening prayers he would break the fast with a hunk of bread and some onion or a bowl of yogurt. Were Khanjan to place some on his doorstep, he would tell her, 'That's wasting food, daughter!'

He had prayed his noon prayers at the neighborhood mosque, shuffling there in the shade and shuffling back home in the shade. The mosque, which was about a hundred meters from his house, was the furthest place he would go regularly. After Khanjan brought him home to stay with her, he wouldn't venture outside except to pray at the end-of-Ramadan festivities. Of course, he had his devotees, who would stop in from time to time. Mirza wouldn't let them kiss his hands. He would say to them, 'Love the Lord. One might say that it's good that people still have faith, given all the catastrophes visited upon them in the name of religion and God's book.'

His eyes were always aglow with a kind of hidden vision, and his soul was as crystal clear as water or a mirror, light as air, like human imagination, limitless and free. He had journeyed to cities outside of our world. It was as if he looked around and through objects, albeit like a little child with the capacity to be deceived. He had been touched somehow by holiness, having first come into the world circumcised, head shaved, and umbilicus severed.

9

Mostafa's uncle, Hajj Da'i, wrapped his rosary around his wrist and, pinching the slender middle of an hourglass-shaped tea glass between two fingers, took it from the tray. Then, as he ran his fingers over the bowl filled with lumps of sugar, he sized up his nephew's choice out of the corner of his eye and, deep in his heart, congratulated him on it. Two rose-colored cheeks, bright Turkmen eyes, an identical pair of moist lips. He could no longer contain himself and said in a loud voice, 'God the Creator be praised!'

Then Shahrzad held out the tray to Khanjan. As she took a glass, Khanjan voiced all sorts of endearments for the charms of her beautiful bride. Hajj Da'i was saying, 'As I entered this house, I said to my sister . . .'

He stopped and looked at Khanjan. Then, holding up a lump of sugar, he asked, 'What did I say, sister? Tell them yourself.'

Khanjan adjusted her chador and laughed with a mixture of affection and reserve. Hajj Da'i moved his head and said, 'Sister, I said, you've brought me to the right door! Yessiree!'

And he put the lump of sugar in his mouth and, sucking on it in obvious pleasure, he went on waggling his head.

Mehri bent her head and, staring at the patterns in the carpet, said, 'What can I say, Hajj Aqa?'

She shook herself. At this point Shahrzad was holding the tray out to Mostafa. Under the gaze of those several pairs of eyes, which no doubt were watching him closely, he didn't dare look at the girl's face; and only at the last moment, when his nostrils were filled with the fragrance that wafted from under Shahrzad's chador, did he look up and fix his eyes on hers. There was a particular warmth emanating from them.

The picture window of the room faced Mecca and looked out on the yard; the slanting light of the late afternoon illuminated a niche in the wall. A thick carpet of poor quality with colors that ran into one another, and that was too large for the sunny room, was bunched up a little at the foot of the wall; the white strands of the fringe lay like braids of hair covering the border, and seemed as if they had been carefully arrayed one by one.

Making a noise, Hajj Da'i took out the lump of sugar from under his teeth and said, 'Last night I said to my sister that a girl who's had no father appreciates the value of a husband more, can better put up with his shortcomings and strong points—didn't I, sister?'

He turned toward Khanjan. She shifted around, smiled, and blinked *yes* kindly.

Hajj Da'i declared, 'Whatever happens, we're not going through that door until we hear a "yes" loud and clear from you.'

Here he stopped talking and pointed to the door. Khanjan again shifted her broad bottom and, without thinking, opened her chador and closed it again.

The room was quiet; no one picked up the thread of the conversation. Hajj Da'i had put his rosary in his pocket, then, as if realizing he had made a mistake, took it out hastily. Mehri still had her head bent, staring at the pattern in the carpet, as if something was supposed to happen among the arches of opal-colored flowers dancing prettily toward the central medallion. After a long pause, she said, 'What can I say, Hajj Aqa?'

Then, holding the hem of her chador over her face, she said something to Shahrzad, who had just sat down next to her, and the girl got up again.

Mostafa looked at the girl, whose chador was now pulled back to reveal a fine gold chain around a crystalline patch of rosy throat covered by downy hair. The girl opened her lips as if to sigh or, at least, that was what Mostafa imagined. Whatever the case, he pulled himself up and, as he was drawn unconsciously toward the gentle breath emerging from Shahrzad's lips, Khanjan poked him in the side with her elbow, and Hajj Da'i coughed. Mehri went on, '. . . That's right, Hajj Aqa! I raised Shahrzad without a father, but I never let it upset her: whatever she wanted, I provided what I could. I denied myself so she could have enough to eat! And now she's yours; a person works her head off to raise a girl, and in the end there's no denying that she's got to give her to others so they can take her away!'

Seemingly choked up, she stopped, dried her eyes with her fists, and sighed, resigned to her fate. Then she shuddered and sighed again; sitting around the old carpet the way they were, with only a couple of woven flowers separating them in that room—how much of the house was it?—hearing their breathing or their hearts beating was nothing; if anyone blinked, they'd sense it.

The niche had a velvet coverlet with two corners decorated with embroidered birds and flowers, and a border of white embroidery. There was a mirror with two yellowed pictures stuck in the frame, and two lapis-colored porcelain vases adorned with two gilded leaves on their bellies—these were the sole ornaments in the room. Of course there was also a framed picture that . . .

Shahrzad picked up plates from the niche and, with the clanking sound they made still in the air, placed them one by one before the guests. The fragrance that again escaped from her collar and, naturally, from her cleavage drove Mostafa crazy; his heart raced, and his mouth went dry. He blinked a few times.

Now Shahrzad was passing around the sweets on a plate, stopping at each guest. When she reached Mostafa, he straightened up.

Hajj Da'i was going on again, 'I don't want to sing the boy's praises'—here he leaned forward and pointed to Mostafa—'he's my sister's boy, after all, but what can I tell you about his noble character? Of course, you can find that out for yourselves.'

He had gotten to the nub of the matter and, feeling both satisfied with himself and relieved, leaned back against the wall.

Khanjan said, 'I was always afraid he would fall into the clutches of one of those girls that loiter in the streets twenty-four hours a day. You yourselves know how hard it is to bring up young people at this time.'

Then, as if she had finally revealed a great mystery, she suddenly let her shoulders drop and relaxed.

Hajj Da'i was emboldened; he touched his sister's shoulder gently and said, 'My nephew is far too clever to do anything like that, sister!'

Everybody laughed. Hajj Da'i shifted his weight, coughed a few times in a row, cleared his throat, shifted again, then thanked God and said, 'The fact of the matter is that these two young people have found it in their hearts to love each other; the rest is just window dressing!'

Mehri said, 'Sure, but I have to say that I raised this girl to be respected, and I wish her to remain that way. I don't want everybody in the neighborhood and the relatives to think that just because she doesn't have a father, somebody can have her for a few pounds of sweets.'

Hajj Da'i said, 'A few pounds of sweets? We are asking you for her in earnest! What are you talking about?'

Both sides were silent, but Hajj Da'i was still on the alert. Then he had to look up and face Mehri, and he said, 'Fine, good lady, please, your comments are most welcome; no matter what, we must take our finances into consideration. Please, state your reservations or conditions!'

Mehri said, 'Shahrzad's uncle was supposed to be in Tehran today, but yesterday he called to say that he was tied up, and he was sorry. The truth of it is that I was too shy to tell you that I wanted to postpone the meeting . . . It didn't hurt to sit around and have tea, anyway.'

Hajj Da'i said, 'This sitting around is fine—brings us closer together. But it wouldn't be right to have these two young people wait longer. Without any more discussion, we'd like to have these two hitched before the month of Moharram comes around.'

Two doves, presumably drunk on the spring air, fluttered in Shahrzad and Mostafa's eyes; they would never get enough of one another with such looks.

Mehri said, 'It's only the middle of Shawwal, Hajji Aqa!'

Hajj Da'i said, 'Fine, but how long is it to Moharram? Before you know it the two months will be over!'

Mehri said, 'The truth is that Shahrzad's uncle told me to ask what the boy does for a living, how much he makes. I told him, all I know is: he is not a shopkeeper, he's an office worker.'

Then she looked from Hajj Da'i to Khanjan.

Hajj Da'i put his hands on his knees, and, looking a few times at Mostafa and from Mostafa to Khanjan, struggled with something on the tip of his tongue. Finally he said, 'Mostafa is the unknown soldier!'

Khanjan said, 'He makes enough to buy groceries, whatever it is. Whatever I have, I mean, is Mostafa's; I have no other children.'

Mehri said, 'Shahrzad's uncle is coming to Tehran on Wednesday so he can stop in at preacher Sheikh Mortaza's to consult the Qur'an for us and find out more about where young master Mostafa works.'

Then she turned to Shahrzad and said, 'Darling, bring us some paper so master Mostafa can write down his address for us.'

Hajj Da'i said, 'You don't need to do that. It's simple: Evin Prison.'

As if startled, Mehri said, 'Evin Prison?'

Hajj Da'i nodded and said, 'You can ask anybody in Tehran. They'll take you straight to the prison. Could there be any address more reliable?'

Mostafa said, 'My boss's name is Mr. Keramat. Tell them that it's about a blessed event. If you'd be kind enough to give me the day of your visit, I'll tell reception myself not to keep you waiting.'

Then, to hide her shock, Mehri asked, 'It must be hard, the work that you do there?'

'Yes, it *is* hard,' Mostafa replied.

He swallowed. Hajj Da'i nodded his head in confirmation and said, 'Yes, good lady, you and I can rest easy at night because there are a few like this Mostafa of ours serving the nation.'

To allow his listeners to appreciate the pure wisdom he had just imparted, Hajj Da'i kept nodding his head for a while, and looked them in the eye one by one. After evaluating what Hajj Da'i said, Mehri stared at him for a moment, then she nodded and said, 'Master Mostafa works at night, then!'

Hajj Da'i immediately said, 'No!'

By this he meant that her conclusion was irrelevant. Mehri nodded without thinking, which contrasted with the confused look on her face. Khanjan said, 'It rarely happens that they keep him there overnight.'

Mehri was bewildered, but tried not to show it. She turned to Mostafa and asked, 'Do you work in the office, or . . .?'

Mostafa said, 'When a person's intentions are pure, madam, it doesn't matter what he does. We all do what we can there.'

With the same uncertain look on her face, Mehri nodded, but this time more slowly, and once again gesturing with her chador, said something to Shahrzad, who had left the room and returned with a tray of fresh tea. As she went around serving the tea, that same scent and that breath made Mostafa light-headed. It was as if most of the air had left the room, or . . . The girl's look was a combination of cowed and restless; that was it! Despite it all, she managed to blink slowly, as if to say, *Come!*

Hajj Da'i took the tea glass from his lips, moved a lump of sugar around in his mouth, and said, 'Madam, would you be so kind as to give me your views—if you have them—on the bride price and the groom's contribution.'

Mehri said, 'The truth is that I haven't spoken with Shahrzad's uncle about what would be best. You know that he's the girl's elder.'

Khanjan said, 'Of course, he's our elder also.'

She slurped tea from her saucer.

Three tea glasses clinked one after another as they were placed on the saucers. Then Hajj Da'i looked around and gestured to Khanjan that it was time to go. He said *Ya Ali*, and everybody stood up; then they left the room.

A few yellow sheets were blowing on the clothesline on one side of the garden, while on the other the steady drip from a spigot made a hole in the earth, and, as they were passing through the postage-stamp-sized compound, Hajj Da'i said, 'Please, if you will, tell the uncle from me that one doesn't use the Qur'an for omens for a blessed event.'

Mehri looked up at the sky and said resignedly, 'Hajj Aqa, it's kismet, whatever is kismet, will happen!'

She said 'happen' with such emphasis and certainty that Mostafa immediately pictured himself in the marriage bed.

Reaching the compound door, they cut the conversation short and didn't tarry as long as etiquette might have required. After Mehri and Shahrzad had closed the door behind them, Mostafa looked around and went on ahead. He spat angrily on the ground and barked, 'We should have wrapped things up today.'

Hajj Da'i said, 'Don't be in such a hurry, son!'

Mostafa was furious; he banged the palm of his hand with his fist and said, 'If I'd been man enough, I wouldn't have left their house empty-handed!'

Hajj Da'i went over to him, took his hand and said, 'Let me give you a piece of advice or two, young man, for times like these . . .'

Mostafa closed his eyes and said, 'I don't need advice! I would have thought that my elders would be interested in moving this thing forward for me, but . . .'

Hajj Da'i said, 'Listen, dear boy!'

Mostafa was almost shouting, 'I'm not a boy!'

Da'i grabbed him by the arm, but more gently than before and said, 'Try to see what I'm telling you.'

Mostafa raised his voice again. 'That's not necessary!'

Khanjan finally bellowed, 'Don't argue with your elders, boy!'

Mostafa quickened his pace and again went on ahead. He couldn't help himself, what with that crystalline throat, those half-open lips, all in his mind's eye; then with one look he pictured her naked, but in all modesty and innocence, reclining on their marriage bed, and suddenly his body went stiff. The girl wanted him; it was clear from the way she looked at him. He consoled himself by saying that it was only a matter of days—that's all! The uncle was coming to Tehran, and then everything would be okay. It was kismet!

But Hajj Da'i was saying to his sister, 'It's like he was deaf; he didn't hear what she said! Unless and until that old bastard is around to see the boy, finds out about where he works, what good will anything we decide be?'

Mostafa shrugged his shoulders. Hajj Da'i raised his voice and said emphatically, 'There's a method to the way the world works!'

Khanjan adjusted her chador, and followed her brother, who was striding testily toward the street. He may have been mumbling something, or, perhaps, praying under his breath.

10

The uncle arrived from Nahavand on Thursday night, and, because everything was closed on Fridays, he had to wait until Saturday before doing anything. Friday morning Mehri, Shahrzad, and her uncle were sitting in the room around the breakfast cloth talking about 'kismet.' They said if it were not destined, no match would take place; and the uncle told story upon story illustrating the point, while Mehri kept refilling his glass with tea. The examples went on until noon.

Saturday morning, the uncle donned his hat and shawl, put the slip of paper with the address in his hand, and left the house. The groom worked in the northern part of town, which was itself an indication of the importance of his job.

In that area all the streets were wide open, and the girls and women looked as though they were related to the bigwigs, they were so done up and dressed up. An hour later, the uncle found himself in front of a large building. He gave it a long look; its high walls concealed the secrets it held inside. The walls had been made higher, crowned with strings of barbed wire. These added to the grandeur and majesty of the place; but the uncle couldn't figure out what was inside.

A guard emerged from a wooden sentry box, the kind that was next to police stations, and told him not to stand there. The uncle still hadn't said what he wanted, and, even after he told him, it didn't seem to make any difference. He didn't let him in; then someone came asking, 'You're the one who wants to know about Mostafa Bahadori?' The uncle nodded. They brought him inside the building, which was like a city in itself with people coming and going. They continued walking until the escort stopped in front of another building and said, 'It's here, second floor, the door facing the stairway.'

Then he left. The uncle looked up. On the front of the building there were several narrow, blue-colored tiles with inscriptions that had been chiseled away. The uncle went inside and stood waiting in the room opposite the stairway.

Behind the closed door of the small room there was a man walking back and forth. Doors opened and closed, hinges creaked, bits of conversation hovered in the hallway, and there were sounds of people rifling pages, and of footsteps. The uncle yawned. He turned around and looked out the window behind him. About fifteen young girls had been lined up and were being led away. They were blindfold, and each had her hands on the shoulders of the one in front. The girl in front was holding the end of a pencil; the other end was in the hands of young man with a bushy beard. He would occasionally turn around and glance at the troop of prisoners. The uncle shook his head and said to himself, 'Poor creatures!'

Disturbed, he stood up and put his sweaty palms on the window. They passed by him, and the uncle, slowly turning his head, followed them until they were out of sight. He felt frustrated and returned to where he had been sitting when the door opened and a heavyset man entered the room, stirring the air. The uncle looked up.

Keramat asked, 'Somebody here looking for me?'

A young man sitting behind a table pointed to the uncle saying, 'Him. The one related to Mostafa Bahadori, the one you yourself mentioned!'

Seeing the heavyset man, of course, took the uncle by surprise, but Keramat greeted him like an old friend he hadn't seen in years; he hugged the uncle and kissed him left and right on the cheek. Then he started praising Mostafa's merit and learning to the skies, his physical capacity for work, his modesty and virtue. He went on for quite a while, and then suddenly stopped speaking. The uncle, who was persuaded by Keramat's ardor, asked finally, 'Mr. Mostafa, what does he actually do here?'

Keramat merely said, 'Everything,' and then ordered tea. Although Keramat had stopped speaking, the uncle was still nodding that he understood. It wasn't long before a stooped old man brought the tea. The uncle offered to help him, but the old man scowled and, having swiftly put the tray on a ledge, handed one glass to the uncle and another to Keramat. Lumps of sugar were placed on the saucers beside the glasses.

Keramat invited the uncle to drink and then downed the tea himself in one gulp. Then he got to the heart of the matter saying, 'If I had ten girls ready for marriage, the one thing I would want from God would be to present them with both hands to Mostafa.'

Then he put his two hands together and extended them toward the uncle. The uncle held his glass from his lips and rolled the sugar around in his mouth. He looked first at

Keramat's two empty hands and then hastily nodded in agreement. Keramat wagged his finger in the air and repeated, 'All ten of them! That would be the thing I would most want from God!'

The uncle's eyes were as wide as saucers, and he drew back. Since a bigwig envied him for his good fortune, without knowing it, he smiled in satisfaction.

Now that there was no mistake that he had won over the uncle, Keramat grew bolder and declared, 'Yes, my dear sir. You bet!'

He puffed out his chest and held his head high. The uncle finished his tea and put the glass on the table; he leaned forward toward Keramat and, sensing a kind of victory, asked, 'His income . . . how much does he bring home?'

As he said this he rubbed the fingers of his right hand together in front of Keramat. Keramat first gave the uncle a good, long look. Then all of a sudden he closed his eyes, put his head back and, with the mass of flesh on his body jiggling, let out a laugh. The uncle, feeling vexed and ashamed, stared at Keramat, but before the laughter stopped, he also started to giggle.

The two men now sat opposite each other laughing; Keramat was, of course, oblivious, and kept on laughing, but the uncle would occasionally open his eyes to size up the situation; but then, of course, he would burst out laughing again until they were both silent.

Keramat wiped his mouth with the side of his hand and said, 'This young man has put his life on the line for the likes of you and me, my dear Hajji. What does how much he makes have to do with anything?'

Then he kept shaking his head regretfully, and let out one or two *heh*s, which was to say that people didn't appreciate the value of those boys who volunteered to sacrifice their lives. Then he let out a few more *heh*s.

Humbled, the uncle smiled and stared at the ground in embarrassment. But a moment later he asked, 'Are you his boss?'

Keramat let out a deep sigh and, straightening his back, stared at the uncle through narrowed eyelids and nodded slowly. Like a chastened child, the uncle first looked at his fingernails, then at the muddy tips of his shoes, and said under his breath, 'God Almighty!'

As if this wasn't enough to satisfy him, he raised his head and repeated, 'God Almighty!'

Then there was silence. The uncle, smiling guilelessly, of course, would look up from time to time and glance at Keramat, at which point his smile would widen; but Keramat remained silent, waiting like a genuine bigwig, soberly.

The uncle shook himself and wanted to say something like, 'Sorry to have caused so much trouble,' or 'Let me go and lessen the bother I caused you,' but found himself—not knowing why—saying, 'Can I take a look at him for myself?'

Keramat drew back and narrowed his eyes; the uncle, looking more apologetic than before, said, 'Just one look!'

Keramat moved further away, which made his face even more awe-inspiring. The uncle pondered Keramat and murmured another 'God Almighty!'

As Keramat's silence dragged on, the uncle had no choice but to say, 'I won't take much of his time!'

Sensing it was the moment to go on the offensive, Keramat blurted out, 'What? In all this time you have yet to see the groom?'

The uncle's shame and embarrassment was now beyond all reason, and, as Keramat regarded him with that same air of superiority, the uncle screwed up his courage and nodded. Keramat erupted. The force of his laughter caused his entire body to shake. The flab draped over every part of his frame jiggled even more, and it seemed as though the jiggling of that massive form filled the entire room; tears streamed down his cheeks. The uncle laughed with him, exclaiming, 'God Almighty! God Almighty!'

And he kept saying that in a loud voice, with no regard for form. Suddenly Keramat became silent. He rose, and, wiping the tears from his face, said, 'Don't go away; I'll send him out!'

The uncle hastily said, 'Naturally!'

If the truth be known, however, he was a little taken aback by Keramat's peremptory tone, though he was certain that he hadn't meant anything by it. Bosses always used this tone. Keramat left the room, and it was as if his exit released a sort of trapped energy; the muscles in the uncle's face relaxed, but then he very quickly looked around in embarrassment, not knowing what to do next. He was, to be sure, a little afraid. He turned and saw another line of people: boys this time, blindfold, again each with his hands on the shoulders of the boy ahead of him. They were being led to a bus with windows covered by thick curtains.

They had blindfolded them! The uncle didn't see the reason for it; all the young men seemed alike to him. When you eliminate the eyes from the face of a person, he loses his physical identity; the uncle knew this instinctively, which was probably why he asked under his breath, 'Where are they taking the poor creatures?'

Suddenly the door opened, causing the uncle to turn around. For some reason he imagined that one of the blind-fold young men, who had somehow left the line, was standing before him, wanting to explain why they were blindfold and where they were being taken—as if he had realized that the uncle was truly worried about them.

Finally the young man said, 'I'm Mostafa!'

The uncle tried to say something, but couldn't, he was so choked up. He struggled, and finally, like someone who has just awakened from a nightmare, asked in terror, 'Where are they taking you, my dear boy?'

He hid his face in the crook of his arm and started crying uncontrollably, his gaunt shoulders heaving madly. Mostafa got the creeps.

11

What's the use of the past? Why can't we just let it go and forget it? Memories from childhood and youth—sullied by the poverty and filth of the age though they may be—can originate in a sincere heart; and if they do they can sow the bright seeds of truth. Those eyes were a remote and dormant memory, suddenly awakened by the eyes Fattah had seen in the rearview mirror. He recalled the pictures from glossy magazines and the posters covering the walls of all the teahouses of Tehran! Later on, when he started frequenting the whorehouses of the city, once again it was her pictures that enlivened those pathetic little rooms and those tiny, covered compounds lit by colored lights; he bought all the magazines, cutting out pictures of her and pinning them to the walls.

But there was one other thing that brought him closer to Shahrzad, a kind of unprecedented sympathy, originating from poverty, or fatherlessness . . . Yes, not having a father; and it felt as if everybody in the city suffered from being without a father. Mothers, yes—a person could always rely on his mother—but fathers, they were a person's bloodline or, at least, that's what people said; a person without a father had no lineage, and fathers were always absent, so a person could never be sure that the man he called 'Dad' was actually his father. This was something, however, that one couldn't think about; it was forbidden to have such thoughts. Fattah remembered the time his mother had said, 'This man is your dad; he's returned, returned from a trip. I told you that he would come back to us in the end.' He bought him ice cream, cotton candy, and filled his pockets with raisins and dried chickpeas; he even taught him how to wrestle. How they wrestled! There was no mistaking that. Sometimes his father would come home from work early and send Fakhri to a neighbor's house. Then they would get naked and grapple with each other. He taught him all the techniques: from the crotch lift and the headlock to the bridge, the half nelson, the cross cradle, and the face push; he taught him how to take down an opponent who was on all fours, and one who was on one hand and one leg, or how to break his bridge or kick his legs out from under him. The first thing they practiced was the between-the-legs takedown; Hasan Khanom grabbed Fattah by the ankles, bringing his legs together, and then, with the boy's twisted legs pinned to the ground, he'd mount him with his own legs. He also taught Fattah variations on every move; he took control of his legs, scissor-kicked him, locked his feet, got him to bridge, or hooked him on his back and pinned him; then he fell to the ground, exhausted.

Fattah always won; he put his hand between his legs, and a filmy substance like snot, but with a pungent smell, would make his fingertips gleam. It was after he reached puberty that he learned what that film was.

Fattah grew up having been taken under the wing of such a man; granted, he wasn't much of a scholar, having left high school before it was half over. Hasan Khanom took him by the hand to Aq Ebram's liquor store. He told Aq Ebram, 'Treat him like your own son!'

He would deliver orders right to the customers' doorsteps. He was an eager beaver who kept his nose clean; at the end of each week he gave every penny he earned to his mother. All he did in his free time was go to the Friday-night movies or dawdle a bit around the recreation places by Tajrish—that was it.

A father is a person's bloodline. Hasan Khanom hailed from the Sampaz Khaneh quarter and worked as a big wholesaler in the fruit and vegetable market. He would stand at the upper part of the square and collect 'entrance fees.' His business prospered; the buttons on his coats were gold. No one had seen the likes of his hospitality; he gave till the cows came home. He sent platters of cookies and cakes to anyone holding a wedding that were so big they didn't go through the door; so they lay them down right there in the alley where the women would come and fill the folds in their chadors with the sweets. The only thing was that he had a temper and was quick to pull out his knife; there wasn't a punk in the bazaar without nicks and cuts from Hasan Khanom's blade, and, despite all the brawls, there wasn't a scratch on his body. These were things his mother had told him about his father. But how can one trust mothers when they tell stories about fathers?

No one knew about Hasan Khanom's origins. He never said a thing about where he came from, but he and God knew how hard his childhood was. His father had died, leaving him a single camel; the little imp led the animal to Yazd where he got some pomegranates, then sold them at the Pamenar market in Tehran—that was before the wholesale market was moved to the Amin al-Soltan district. By the time he was eighteen or nineteen, he had become strong enough to tear a copper tray with his bare hands and bend a brass coin with two fingers. Even the big goons in Tehran gave him a wide berth. He was still fairly young when he pulled down the Lion and Sun emblem from the entrance to the local constabulary, thus making a name for himself, and, because he was good-looking, he gradually earned his nickname, 'Miss Hasan.' In those days his job was chasing ass on Lalehzar Avenue. His best friend was Mehdi 'the Sheep's Head and Trotter Man,' whom the Russians killed after the coup. He was always mentioning this, and each time he did, it would pain him so much he wouldn't say a word until nightfall. But he might sing a few songs—he had a fine voice—always taken from classical poems. At the entrance to the Ferdous Gardens, there was a teahouse, where he would sit during the evening. When he sang, sparrows flocked to the trees and immediately stopped chirping; these were things he told Fattah after the boy had reached the age of reason.

Hasan Khanom also worked out at a traditional gym called a 'house of strength'; he tossed and twirled the huge bowling-pin-shaped barbells and raised weighted shields; he had broad shoulders. His chest was buff, his biceps massive; he always wore a gold coin around his neck. During those years, he also got tattooed from his fingers to his chin. He had a crown flanked by two scimitars, a woman with curly locks, a coiled dragon waiting to strike. There were poems too about the brevity of life and the unreliability of this world, about the beauty of the beloved and her cruelties, about the heartache caused by her tresses and her dart-like lashes. He was also master of the entry bell; anytime he set foot in a house of strength, the leader would ring it for him.

He started out as the standard-bearer for the Sha'ban holy procession group; he also carried the mirrored crown for them. Later on, after he had married Fakhri and repented, he formed his own procession group, set up a prayer tent, and held passion plays in honor of the Holy Imams. It didn't take long for him to become the patron of the biggest group of passion-players in Tehran, with a thousand members thumping their chests, and four hundred beating themselves with chains—hallelujah!

His tent was set up on one of the corners of Amin al-Soltan Square two days before the month of Moharram, when they commemorated the martyrdom of Hoseyn at Karbala. From the first day to the night of the tenth, men beat their chests. Hasan Khanom hoisted the standard himself and marched out of the tent. Crowds of people would leave their homes, blocking the streets in the area. Men tied their shirts around their waists and thumped their naked chests, spattering blood on the ground; they struck themselves with true passion—this was no pretend ceremony.

Hasan Khanom's group stretched from the grain store all the way to Cyrus Street. They got under way, passing several places until they reached the execution grounds. When they got to Mowlavi Avenue, the group disbanded. A God-fearing soul, Hasan Khanom swore to the standard-bearer of Karbala that he'd give up alcohol during the months of Safar and Moharram.

When the Shah's son was born, the wholesale market was festooned with colored lights. Hasan Khanom received a Colt pistol from the Shah. The anti-royalists started to chastise him, saying, 'Be careful you don't wind up in hell for nothing!' Hasan Khanom cried and kissed their hands, seeking forgiveness. Around that time Gina Lollobrigida visited Iran, and a thug named Sha'ban the Brainless gave her a small carpet, which outraged people's sense of dignity. There was an attempt on Sha'ban's life, which, of course, was not successful, but at least they paralyzed his hand. Part of the dispute stemmed from the monopoly on bananas that the Shah had granted to Sha'ban the Brainless. Whatever the case, if the wholesale market and bazaar had not existed, the Shah wouldn't have collapsed.

Most of all Fattah wanted to know the kind of person Shahrzad's father was. Was he a good man? Had he hurt the innocent child? Had he done anything to harm her? He prayed with all his soul it wasn't the bastard's handiwork that sent the girl to his clinic. How could he have the heart to do that? It was probably for this reason that he picked up Shahrzad near her home every day and brought her to sewing school; he couldn't help himself. She wouldn't say a thing; she only stared. Fattah declared, 'You've changed my life.'

He stamped his feet, moved his head from side to side, and let out a loud sigh; the feeling was so intense and intimate. No one but him could understand its depth and breadth. Then he found himself alone again.

They didn't speak much, if at all; Fattah would merely turn from time to time and, with a particular anguish, stare at her profile. Shahrzad, patient and forlorn, drowned in gray thoughts, only looked out at the street. Fattah said, 'You should say something too, girl!'

What should she say? That he should leave her alone? That he was old enough to be her father? What? He had money, his mobile rang all the time, and he was extremely well connected. There was also this, of course: being with him didn't make her feel bad; it gave her, rather, a dubious sense of security. She had nothing to hide from him, this man, who had touched the most intimate and private parts of her being. This man had gotten closer to her than any other person; there were no secrets between them now.

Part of a person's being belongs to that person alone; but, after a temporary burning sensation, without expecting anything in return, she had shared that secret part with another. Now a claimant had arrived, as if all things were beyond her determining.

On that sunny morning as she got in the car, Fattah turned and said, 'Don't go to class today. I want to show you my home.'

Shahrzad didn't object, reacting as if she hadn't heard what he'd said. Fattah was suddenly very happy. Her silence added to his happiness; he stepped on the gas. Now the cars were the latest models, and what people wore was new. The streets were unfamiliar to Shahrzad.

Then, all at once, they reached the place, and Shahrzad was struck with an absolute numbness. The high-rise's large iron gate had tiles in the pattern of a deer and a bird. Fattah honked, then turned to Shahrzad and said, 'This is your slave's house, meaning it's yours to own.'

Shahrzad was looking at her new home when she heard someone come running from the yard, then an Afghan boy opened the gate. Fattah drove inside.

After following a path that wound its way through the trees, they suddenly entered an enormous underground garage, which was full of columns and which echoed and magnified the slightest sound. Although the garage was full of fleeting shadows and clipped whispers, she wasn't frightened in the dimly lit area.

He held her hand in the garage, but when they got into the elevator, and the door closed and the music began to play, he embraced her, and she suddenly started to tremble, shut her eyes, and said, 'No!'

The man's embrace felt steamy, like a bath, and there arose from a seemingly bare and remote place the faint echo of murmuring; the moment didn't last long, but it made her apprehensive.

The elevator bell rang, indicating that they had reached the twelfth floor. The door opened, and they stepped out. The air was perfumed and Fattah said, 'I adore you. Is that a crime?'

Did this assertion mean anything? He had become young, and Shahrzad saw the youthfulness in his look, the spark in his eyes, the almost imperceptible stirring of his skin, which might open the way for new sensations, make him act like a much younger man. It was in that dark hallway that Shahrzad began to feel afraid. Why had she come? But that was not the issue; things now seemed to be happening from a distance, as though she were recalling remote events quite by accident.

There were two doors off the dimly lit hallway; maybe somebody was behind them.

Fattah whistled as he took his keys from his pocket and opened the door. 'Go!' he said.

His voice was deep, but at the same time shook as if he were already on her. Defenseless, Shahrzad looked around and stepped inside. Even from the entrance she could tell this was a large, luxurious apartment. Fattah closed the door behind him, and Shahrzad automatically turned toward him and said, 'Let me go!'

She said it with some difficulty, but without pleading, without begging, and she was surprised by her reaction.

Fattah laughed. He threw his car keys in the air and caught them.

His eyes glazed over, then he took a good look at her and said, 'Go?' He stepped ahead of her, turned, and, looking behind him, said, 'Come!'

In an Iran where even the most innocent gesture between a man and a woman becomes erotic, this direct expression of sexuality was terrifying.

Fattah took off his jacket, opened a couple of shirt buttons, narrowed his puffy eyes, and once again said, 'Come!'

Shahrzad didn't move. There was a certain mysterious something in the air, which suddenly made itself apparent in the dark corners and the unused nooks of the apartment. Fattah lunged toward her drunkenly, clumsily, and, with his hand on her arm, said, 'Don't be a child!'

This time the fiery current that flowed continuously from the man's hand made her blood run faster and, at the same time, opened a black pit before her.

Fattah reached out and pulled off her head covering. Shahrzad looked down, saying simply, 'No!'

It was just a game. Just a game that always terrified her.

Fattah put his finger under Shahrzad's chin, making her look up, and exhaled the air in his lungs onto the girl's closed eyes. He squeezed her, lifted her off her feet, and with both hands carried her from the foyer and the living room, past a large table with two gold, round lampshades suspended from a long cord over it, into an open kitchen, where white light coming from unseen lamps shone in several directions, intensifying the sheen of the tiles, steel, and crystal. Finally they reached the bedroom, which was like the ones in films, like the pictures from foreign magazines; then he threw her on the bed.

She filled her lungs with air, which was full of metallic particles and the man's bittersweet smell. From behind her closed eyelids she could also sense the glare of the sun, which stripped bare all the objects in the room.

Shahrzad opened her eyes for a second and looked at him. Fattah's knees were on either side of her chest, and his hand was firmly gripping the opening of her cloak, as well as everything underneath it. She put her hands on his and said with a stutter, 'Look . . .!'

Fattah took one swipe at her clothing. The buttons on her coat came off and shot into the air. Shahrzad opened and closed her eyes again—what else was there to do? A pair of cheap pink knickers. He tore those with his hand, then suddenly the red bra on the girl's white skin flashed and a warm wave of her womanly smell robbed Fattah of reason.

Fattah, his hands trembling, undid his belt and pulled his round-necked T-shirt over his head. Searching for a word, Shahrzad, stammering, unable to find the word, finally said, 'No!'

She pushed her elbows against Fattah's slick chest.

Fattah let out an abandoned grunt and said, 'I'll stitch you up again, if you want!'

Fattah's chin was quivering, and his eyes were slightly crossed; he was in another world and this state was an odd one for him. He gently pried Shahrzad's arms back and, saying *whew*, fell on the girl, and the two of them crossed the threshold.

Several minutes later, both of them were lying on their backs. Her mind empty of thought, Shahrzad felt cold and pulled the sheet toward her. It was quiet.

Fattah declared, 'That was wonderful!'

Shahrzad indicated she agreed. Fattah turned toward her and asked, 'Feel okay?'

She didn't feel anything, but nodded in an ambiguous way, as if to say, 'I'm okay,' or something like it.

Fattah said, 'I'm okay, too!'

And he was telling the truth. Then he said, 'This kind of thing happens, after all, sooner or later. What difference does it make?'

He was probably right. Then he laughed for no reason, and uttered the cliché, 'I am at your service!'

12

It was a lovely sunny morning. The sparrows were hopping from branch to branch and chirping on the bare plane trees. Clean-shaven and hair slicked, Fattah took the box of sweets from one hand and put it in the other, lingered, and rang the bell again. His lips rounded, and he was about to whistle when he heard the sound of footsteps behind the door; then he exhaled, straightened himself, and looked around. A woman pulled back the curtain on the window facing him.

The door opened, and Fattah stood to one side. Then, arching his back a bit, he pushed his head through the door.

Shahrzad was shocked to see him, and pulled back.

Fattah said, 'Hello.'

A kind of magnetic pull held her in check for a moment, then released her. Shahrzad closed her eyes; she stood mute behind the door.

Fattah put his hand on the door, and, with a twinkle in his eye and a smile on his lips, he lowered his voice to a deep bass and said, 'I came to get what you owe me!'

His clammy breath struck her face. There was a kind of blunt sexuality in the way he spoke and the way he looked at her, which drove the bass note in his voice even deeper. Tormented by his directness, Shahrzad started to breathe heavily, and murmured, 'Owe?'

She had trouble speaking, and could only stare at the ground.

Fattah's face brightened, and he nodded his head in triumph. The same sensuality—this time even more unmistakable than before—exuded from the pores in his face; then, with the tone of voice people use to tease children, he said, 'You owe me some tea, remember?'

Fattah was still smirking sarcastically. Shahrzad's shoulders dropped, and she smiled, breathing a sigh of relief; but she wouldn't come out from behind the door. She fixed her radiant eyes on the man.

Fattah pushed against the crack in the door and asked, 'So, I can come in . . . No?'

Shahrzad wasn't sure; the only way to describe her state would be to call it helpless.

At that point, from the doorway of her room, Mehri shouted, 'Who's there, Shahrzad?'

Shahrzad turned toward the voice, and, before she could respond, Fattah entered. Then Shahrzad retreated saying, 'Kindly come in, please!'

Fattah walked inside with exaggerated steps. His booming voice echoed, rattling the house to the rafters: 'Guests aren't welcome here?'

Mehri hurriedly threw on her chador.

Fattah was sitting cross-legged at the far end of the room, leaning on a pillow, and, with his eyes fixed on the carpet, said, 'They wouldn't allow it, ma'am, they wouldn't! We were very naive, imagining that a few years after we had gotten rid of the Shah, the country would become heaven on earth, but it didn't. They wouldn't let it. Before we realized what was happening and took action, they had unleashed the anti-revolutionary groups on the Revolution. We had not finished with them when that bastard Saddam attacked; now, of course, the revolutionary forces are doing their job, but it's going to take years before they can fix the damage.'

He said the last sentence with a mixture of hope and fear, then grew silent, probably waiting for his voice to regain its vigor.

Mehri arranged her chador tight around her face and nodded agreeably. After Fattah stopped, she sighed and said, 'We are content with what God commands.'

She looked at the ceiling and nodded again.

Perhaps aware that defeat was a certainty, Fattah lowered his voice and said, 'We imagined that we could export our revolution, but now, instead of revolution, we're exporting boatloads of our daughters through the port of Bandar Abbas to Dubai; instead of making a revolution, we contribute to the prosperity of the world's whorehouses! Dear lady, my heart aches, this girl, like a bouquet of roses . . .'

He stopped. The sound of footsteps came from the hallway, and both of them looked toward the door, then at each other. Fattah blurted out, 'I won't beat around the bush, dear lady, I have seen your daughter and fallen in love. Today I come to ask for her hand: simple as that!'

He moved and then exhaled loudly.

Mehri didn't move, speak, or look up; she stared at the pattern in the carpet. She knew what he wanted; she had had a premonition. The day he drove them from the clinic to their doorstep, she saw how he stared at Shahrzad, and it put fear in her heart. She didn't know what it was about him that bothered her. Was it because he had had his hands between her darling daughter's thighs? But he wasn't the one who called on them; they came to him out of choice, and Batul had begged and pestered him so much he brought the date of the operation forward. Mehri felt as if all the troubles of the world were at her doorstep. It was her fault, she said to herself, and wondered what cursed misery would she have to go through to atone for it.

Fattah said, 'I swear by my creed and faith, it would be a shame for that daughter of yours to rot in this wreck of a house!'

Then he glanced all around the place and banged his fist on the wall. 'There's not much separating this dump from the wrecking ball, which is what it deserves!'

Something caved in when the man hit the wall with his fist. Mehri drew back as if she herself had been hit.

Fattah said, 'See?'

Mehri was silent again; then she sighed.

Fattah said, 'I told myself that if I didn't act fast, they'd give the girl to some bum of a husband!'

He suddenly thrust his hand behind his head as if to show somebody had gotten her and was now carrying her off.

Perhaps trying to summon the nerve to speak, Mehri closed her eyes and, pleading, but at the same time irritated, said, 'This wretched daughter of mine already has a hard-as-nails suitor who's never going to give up, I swear!'

Fattah turned halfway toward her, and, his eyebrows shooting up, he looked at the woman out of the corner of his eye and said, 'What suitor, dear lady? This girl should live happily ever after. Don't talk about other suitors.'

He stopped, but there was still a look of disapproval on his face that radiated on the air, which, it seemed, was getting thicker by the minute.

Outside the room, Shahrzad was leaning against the wall with her eyes closed. A temporary dizziness came to her from some faraway place, and she felt a wave of agitation that had begun in her legs, and was now rippling through her shoulders.

Mehri said in a detached voice, 'First we have to see what she wants, Doctor. After all, she's not a child!'

This seemed a reasonable excuse; her words had a calming effect. Fattah looked down for a moment, and then, opening his eyes wider and, in a low voice that only Mehri could hear, said in a tone full of mutual understanding, 'Bravo!'

His dark eyes flashed, and he leaned forward; then, more softly than before, he said, 'Girls nowadays are not the innocents you were in your day, madam!'

Then he raised his head a few times. Mehri looked into his eyes for a moment; there was a peculiar flush in that insolent look. Then, lowering his tone even further, he said, 'Take it from me, madam, the girls these days want a man, a real *man!*'

The last word echoed through the room, making Mehri feel even more insecure.

Fattah drew back and leaned against the wall; he had a sweet, lustrous smile on his face. Then he nodded, and, as if thrilled by a new discovery, repeated, 'A man!'

The word reverberated in the air, this time coming to life as a figure with wooly chest hair, tattoos, and muscles slick with sweat; the unbridled lust of the man had now left his eyes and leached into his speech.

Not knowing what to say, Mehri nodded and looked around despairingly.

Fattah made a face as if he had just smelled something awful and said, 'Who is this prince of a suitor? No doubt he's one of these dirt-poor kids that are so common nowadays!'

As he said this, he moved his hands in the air in a disparaging way. There was a note of malice and anger in his voice.

Mehri tilted her head and, in a sympathetic and forgiving voice, said, 'He's one of God's creatures, too!'

Fattah shrugged and, in a hurtful tone, said, 'What am I, good lady, the spawn of the Devil? I'm one of God's creatures also!'

As if aided by a sudden new strength on their uneven playing field, Mehri raised her head and declared stubbornly, 'But the other one's more like us!'

Fattah shook himself and repeated what the woman had said with a sarcastic smile, *'That one's more like us!'*

Then he became serious and raised his voice a notch. 'You shouldn't do this, because if you do, very soon you'll regret it and then you'll ask, "What should I do now?" Do you have something against her eating regularly?'

He shook his head, hiding the malice in his words. But his vicious tone emboldened Mehri; she straightened her head and, with a show of detachment, said, 'When the groom is like us, then my daughter won't have to put up with the humiliation of being without and unable to do anything about it!'

Fattah leaned forward and, in a way that showed both want and hurt, said, 'Who's talking about humiliation, good lady? God willing, if fate will have it, my mother will come and you will see her; she's just like you, having raised me by herself. Of course, I made something of myself, working my butt off for the Revolution, and now I've got something to show for it. I've got to tell you, money means no more to me than the mud on my hands. Tomorrow we'll come and put everything we have on the table and then disappear under a ton of dirt—and that'll be that!'

With that, he held his hands in the air and brushed them off.

Mehri said, 'True, but . . .'

Fattah didn't give her the chance to finish. 'You know, this daughter of yours is precious! Who'd have the nerve to abase her that way?'

Then he raised his head and looked at the half-open door to the room. A shadow passed and, a moment later, warmth that could only have emanated from the body of a girl rippled through the room. Every atom in the man's body began to gravitate in that direction. Then, to put the finishing touch to his argument, he said, 'I'll never give up!'

That was exactly what Mehri was afraid of.

13

As soon as Fattah arrived he raced to the refrigerator, removed a pitcher of water, and drank it down.

Fakhri said, 'You're drinking chilled water in cold weather like this? Have you got dropsy, or something?'

Ignoring her, Fattah put the pitcher back, closed the refrigerator, and said, 'Mom, you'd better get ready, because one of these days you're going to have a bride and grandkids!'

This was the umpteenth time he had said this! Fakhri rolled her eyes, saying, 'That's a hope I'm just going to take to my grave, I know!'

Fattah slapped himself on the jaw and said, 'I'll be damned if I don't. I'm telling you: this time it's for real!'

Fakhri looked her son up and down; it wasn't just his face or the way he held himself that reminded her of that brief, remote passion from her past. Everything about her son was like him, as if he had been farted right out of his father's behind. There wasn't a dime's worth of difference between them.

Fattah got on his knees before his mother and kissed her forehead. 'Then I'll have to start thinking about finding an available young man from a good family for you, Mama!' he said mockingly.

Rather than smiling, Fakhri frowned. 'Shame on you!'

'Well, is that against religion or something? What's the harm?' said Fattah defensively.

Fakhi moved her hands in the air as if swatting a fly and said, 'Mind your own business!'

Fattah puffed himself up and said solicitously, 'Right, until now that's all I've been thinking about, which has made me ignore you; but from now on it'll be different!'

He wagged his finger in the air by way of warning, and he started to laugh, rocking his huge bulk.

The bed creaked as Fakhri rose, moaning and groaning, and, as she dragged herself on her two swollen feet to the samovar, asked him, 'You want tea?'

Fattah got up but didn't answer. Fakhri turned toward him. Fattah pushed out his chest, put his hands in his pockets, and paced up and down the room as though the entire universe owed him something.

Fakhri said, 'I asked you . . .'

Fattah, naturally, wasn't listening; then he said suddenly, 'It was worth waiting ten or fifteen years for a daughter-in-law; you've got to put her on a pedestal so all the neighbors can come and see her.' Then he let out a whoop at the top of his lungs and rubbed his hands together.

Fakhri said, 'Sit down for a second and tell me who she is. Where did you find her?'

Fattah said, 'I told you already! Didn't I? I've been so head-over-heels in love for a month it's made no difference to me whether it's night or day.'

Fakhri took a good look at Fattah; he had lost a little weight.

Fattah made a fist with one hand and put it in the other. He bent toward his mother and said, 'This is no woman, Mom; she's a salve for my heart. That's why I'll put her right here!'

He pounded his chest a few times. Then he kissed his mother on the cheek. Fakhri moaned again and was going back to bed when Fattah said playfully, 'Let me carry you piggyback, Mommy!'

He went to lift her on his back, and Fakhri started to grunt and groan.

If throbbing pain shot through Fakhri's body from the tips of her toes to the top of her head, or if she squawked from time to time because she hurt everywhere, it was because she had spent a lifetime breaking her back. She had sacrificed heart and soul to the Revolution.

In the beginning, she was a Revolutionary Sister; then she was promoted to Revolutionary Mother. She had gotten a full education in what it meant to be revolutionary, dealing first with the SAVAK agents, then graduating to the political groups, the poorly veiled, the liberals, and the Bani Sadrists. Then came the Spy-nest US Embassy, the Cultural Revolution, the Imposed War, all of which were the brainchildren of the Americans. She had, of course, established her revolutionary credentials even before it had begun, from the time that she was no more than a child. At ten or twelve she started to prowl the streets, and, a bit later, found herself a boyfriend; at that young age she was sure, but didn't know why, that having a lover was no sin.

In Hasan Khanom's home she was a reasonable woman. But the story of her frequenting the streets began when one day one of the neighborhood women came to her door and said, 'Come, let's go out and see the demonstrations.' Fakhri asked, 'What are demonstrations?' The neighbor said, 'Come and I'll show you.' They went and walked to the metal gates of the university, but could go no further. Young boys and girls, who would eventually become doctors, engineers, and teachers, were shouting, and a number of guards with truncheons and shields were attacking them. It was like a game, and Fakhri got a kick out of it, shouting with the rest of the women: 'We support the combative students!' and other slogans.

This was to become her life's work. After Fattah and Hasan Khanom had gone off to work, she would put on her chador and go out into the street. The gates to the university opened gradually; students came pouring out and asked the women on the sidewalks to join them. At first, the women hesitated. One explained she had dinner cooking on the stove and was afraid it would burn. Another said she hadn't finished preparing her meat and chickpea mash and was afraid that if she didn't attend to it, her family would starve. Another . . . But it was impossible to make excuses, not with the game going on, and, finally, one by one, they went into the streets.

They formed groups and went on their way. They went out in the morning and returned in the evening. Fakhri shouted so much in the streets that, at sunset when she got home, she had no voice left. Hasan Khanom would ask, 'What has the Shah done to these people that makes them demonstrate against him?' He wouldn't go. But, one night when there was to be a strike the next day, he had a dream. A certain man came to him and gave him a piece of rock candy that had been blessed. Hasan Khanom didn't see his face, and, by the time he turned around, the man had gone. His eyes welling with tears, Hasan Khanom told the dream to everybody. Afterwards he stood firmly with the strikers. He brought a butcher's knife home for protection; once or twice, when people feared that the guards were about to attack, he chose caution and kept the knife with him.

Now, after a twenty- or thirty-year struggle, the cinematic world of people like Fardin, Behruz Vosuqi, and Kimiya'i had at long last emerged from the dark and dilapidated theatres and spilled into the streets; Hasan Khanom was with the people, acting just like a regular movie good guy, beating his chest in solidarity with the martyred Imam, praying, lighting candles at sacred cisterns, and crying at the metal grates around the sepulchers of the holy ones; while the SAVAK agents were playing the parts of the neighborhood thugs, who wanted to pick up our sisters. If they got caught, they would be beaten to a pulp.

Now goodness reigned; the doves ate birdseed on mosque domes, and people filled the five-ton copper chalices with cold water from underground cisterns and drank it down. At the entrance to the mosques and the passion-play houses, there was ululation. People cooked food that guaranteed they would be true to the vows they had made; they sacrificed animals and sprinkled rosewater. Visiting the graveyards, consecrating rock candy, observing the seventh- and fortieth-night ceremonies after the deaths of the martyr, who now belonged to everyone—all of this was a continuation of the cinema of the seventies.

After the victory of the Revolution, Hasan Khanom found a place for himself in it. Then the uprisings began: first in Kurdistan, then Gonbad-e Qabus, then Khorramshahr . . . He'd pack his bag and go, and, once or twice, Fakhri noticed that he had taken his knife with him.

Sedition had broken out in every part of the country. The television said, 'We know who is behind this; they've shown their hands. We're going to lift the curtain to make it clear to the Muslim and revolutionary people who is responsible.'

Fakhri looked at the curtains, afraid that as soon as it was dark someone would jump out from them and scare her to death, or a hand would suddenly emerge from Fattah's jacket, which was hanging on the coat tree, and—God forbid—grab her, and she would be raped. Hasan Khanom had the same anxiety; in fact he, like all the men in the country, was afraid of the loss of honor. He told Fakhri, then, 'Why are you just sitting there, doing nothing?'

He was right. Fakhri put her hands on her knees and, with an O Ali, got to her feet. She said to herself: 'I shouldn't sit around the house staring at the curtains. God would not be pleased if I just watched from the sidelines.'

The women usually gathered in front of the university. They hated the infidel Communist girls so much they could spit. All of these girls had their hair in braids, and, with those newspapers clutched in their fists, they would talk back to the men. For their part, the men, not taking their eyes off the girls' breasts, would say, 'You college-educated tell us: If we throw out the door these bourgeois compradors, whom America protects, and these imperialists, they'll come back through the window and exploit us toiling masses. It would be good if you college girls could teach us what to do.'

Fakhri was forever saying, 'I know what's got the men all hot and bothered, otherwise they wouldn't give a damn about these miserable creatures. What about me? Is there a more pathetic person on earth? Now all of a sudden these sluts are going to recover our rights? They figured wrong!' Then she narrowed her eyes and hissed between clenched teeth, 'I wish to God somebody would hand them over to me. I'd pick apart their bodies with a pair of tweezers so everybody in their families for seven generations back would know how much I hate these infidels. Where do they come off, preaching to me? Up yours, you damned nymphos, you dykes!'

The battles over honor that took place in cafés in the movies now left the big screen and entered the streets. The girls were being beaten to keep immodesty and disgrace from returning to the land. Women were now to have their faces tightly covered, run home, keeping close to the walls, greet one another and ask after their mothers, and mothers were to fill the pockets of their darlings with white jasmine and say seven *God is Great*s. Well, what can one do? Isn't everybody going to end up six feet under with only a shroud to his name?

To make the Communist kids feel ashamed, the Muslim kids stood twice a day in public prayer lines, which stretched from the university mosque to Revolution Street, and spilled into the surrounding alleys. This blocked the streets; cars honked their horns, and passengers in taxis grumbled, 'They'll go to hell. So what if these Muslim kids don't pray their prayers?'

Then they said improperly veiled women had to go; prostitutes would no longer be tolerated. That is why the women, accustomed to living free all their lives, arranged to go to the President's office together to protest, but before the gathering fully formed, a handful charged, and pierced the heavens with the cry: 'Cover up, or get beaten up!' Then the women ran away.

Dressed in a pair of men's boots, with her chador tied behind her head, Fakhri hunted Communist kids. But those kids didn't sit around idly, either; once or twice, having gotten her alone, they gave her a good what for, which made her hate them even more. When the conditions were right, she'd grab them by their braids and hand them over to Keramat and his gang, who hung out around the university. The men would tan the kids' hides so viciously that even their forefathers, long in their graves, would hear about it. Afterwards, of course, she always felt sorry.

One time, when Fakhri was dragging a girl by the hair, it suddenly occurred to her that, eighteen or twenty years before, a woman had given birth to the girl, and she felt something like tenderness, which shook her heart to the core. Well, yes! The mothers had given birth to these girls, women like her, whether downtown or uptown, fortunate or, perhaps, unlucky. Whatever the case, maybe it was because of all the absent women and their dignity that Fakhri suddenly hugged the girl and cried her eyes out.

Fakhri was such a kind-hearted soul she often regretted what she had done. On the other hand, for some unknown reason, she was always embarrassed and depressed. That was why, in every confrontation, she would quickly back down before it erupted into a shouting match. All things considered, she actually liked the Communist girls; it was as if they were her own daughters. Deep in her heart, she wished them happiness, wanted them to be well behaved and obedient, marry good husbands, and bear them several sons. Then she recalled her own fate, and her eyes filled with tears.

Those were the days when the Spy-nest US Embassy was liberated, and Fakhri came into her own. She would remain near the embassy from the crack of dawn to the wee hours of the night. Then one day she borrowed a big brass cauldron from the local prayer hall, and got the neighbors to ante up ingredients for a soup. In the middle of the night, she loaded everything on the back of Mash Hamdollah's son's pickup, brought it to the Spy-nest, and, before sunup, Fakhri's soup was ready.

With fall half over, a chill was in the air, and the young people sat in groups, tending the fires they had made. They were, after all, resting to gather strength for the coming battles with the Hezbollahis, which were to resume a few months later in front of the university.

Above a brick oven set up near the water channel beside the road, thick clouds of steam smelling of turmeric and pepper cut through the chilly air, reaching every part of the area. When the aroma reached the bands of naive young people sitting around, it made their stomachs growl. Then, one by one, they would leave their comrades and drift toward the smell. Over subsequent days, this instinctual response gradually became common practice, without which the great anti-imperialist struggle, designed to rub the 'oppressors' snouts' in the dust, might have been lacking, or even fruitless.

In time, every morning just before dawn, with Fakhri's soup nearing its final stages, a long line would form before the cauldron. It was so long it extended into the darkness of the capital, from the very walls of the Spy-nest to Shemran Gate, the Seyyed Ali Crossroads, and even beyond.

As the young boys and girls stood in line, they talked, and concluded that the soup line was a forceful blow to imperialism; it wouldn't be long, then, before imperialism would be brought to its knees. The American-supported 'liberals' would be thoroughly disgraced.

The fledgling leftists had but one desire: to be eternally anti-American. Despite this, they drank Coke, wore jeans, and watched westerns. Fakhri recalled some of them: they were the same Communist girls, except now their braids were hidden under headscarves, though the ends still stuck out. Everybody, however, was of the opinion that the present regime was rightly and justly called 'anti-imperialist.' Fakhri watched them through narrowed eyes and stirred the cauldron. At these times she had such a thoughtful and determined look one got the feeling she was stirring a proud and mighty nation, that her soups were people making history.

At the beginning of the day the wind blew the cold ashes in Fakhri's oven this way and that. She was washing out the empty cauldron and measuring out the ingredients for the next day's food when the political groups and their grandiose speakers arrived. Fakhri shouldered the paddle she used to stir the soup, shielded her eyes from the sun with her hand, and listened to the speeches. The Shah has taken out American citizenship, they said; he's being operated on in a New York hospital, restoring his circumcized penis to its original state.

They've dubbed him 'David Newsome.' Then the chant of 'Death to David Newsome' rang out, rattling the doors, windows, and even causing the street to shudder.[1] There were the deafening sounds of megaphones, and the crowds ebbed and flowed like a tide twenty-four hours a day.

One of the speakers pointed to Fakhri, who was standing by her cauldron, and said, 'Look how this Muslim sister aids the movement by ladling out home cooking. The damned Shah, in his celebration of twenty-five hundred years of satanic rule, invited all the heads of the oppressor states to Iran but ordered the food from Maxim's of Paris. Even that couldn't put things right!'

At that point, the whole crowd yelled, 'All hail the warrior sister! All hail the warrior sister!'

Another speaker said, 'The horns of oppression blare in their newspapers that we've taken the ingredients of this soup from the embassy kitchen, while the hostages starve. But you know that the people themselves provided the chickpeas and beans. We have even given some to the spies.'

Fakhri marked each round of appreciation by adding more sautéed mint and onions to her soup and, occasionally, threw in some roast garlic, the odor of which, after every single belch—may your face be sprinkled with rosewater—would be like shit on the assembled crowd. As the sit-in gradually

---

[1]On his last trip to America, Mohammad Reza Shah, who was to undergo surgery, used a false passport in the name of 'David Newsome'; but, before he could get to the hospital from the airport, word came that photographers and reporters had gathered at the entrance of New York Hospital.

became an all-day affair, people didn't go home at night to sleep. They were scattered in the alleyways and lanes around the embassy, and soon an unpleasant odor arose that the slightest breeze would transport all over the city.

When it became clear that Fakhri's one cauldron of soup would not be enough, some people had the idea of cooking additional dishes, which would not only help then in honoring their vows, but would feed the protesters at the embassy. As bowls of this food were passed from hand to hand, the crowd rang out in a heaven-piercing chorus of 'Expose the Americans! Expose them!' to the students occupying the embassy. On certain days, of course, people fasted anti-imperialistically; but this didn't lessen Fakhri's workload. She still had to prepare two meals: one for the sundown breaking of the fast, and another for the predawn feeding. The pre-dawn one had to be especially generous so it would stick to people's ribs.

The next year, exactly on the anniversary of the taking of the Spy-nest, the gates of the embassy opened for the public to visit the grounds. Group after group entered, and, on exiting, they said some very odd things. They said the hollows between the trees were where Americans set fire to people and tortured them. There were certain shady characters, however, who listened to these tales in silence, and, when one of them had the temerity to say, 'No, these holes were for burning leaves in the fall,' he received such a brutal beating he was on the verge of death. Even Fakhri gave him a few whacks on the head with her ladle.

Fakhri's business got better and better by the day; everyone hailed her as the 'Soup Mother.' But sometimes a few little brats would find fault with her food, saying it wasn't quite right, or the liquid and beans hadn't melded, or it didn't have enough sautéed mint. Fakhri paid no attention; she wiped her hands on her apron, and, in the manner of the bigwigs, waved the handle of her ladle in the air like a baton and marched on. She was sure that, in time, these complainers would say unanimously that in the whole megacity only Sister Fakhri's soup was perfect.

Truly and honestly, her soup was perfection. After all, she spared no effort making it, meticulously carrying out her soup duties to the letter, always putting it on the stove in the middle of the night, and, once the split peas had become soft, adding the greens. She cooked the rice in a separate pot. Then she mashed and strained it and added it to the cauldron. The resulting steamy broth was beyond compare; its aroma traveled to far-flung neighborhoods, and it was even the talk of the town on the other side of the world! Pictures of the Soup Mother with her paunch and her ample breasts, standing over the cauldron, piping-hot steam pouring from it, adorned the front pages of important newspapers around the globe. The awesome sight of Fakhri and her great cauldron had but one message for oppressed peoples all over the earth: the eradication of world hunger.

It became the favorite pastime in the city for people to make a pilgrimage to the Spy-nest, repent of their sins, and have a ladleful of Mother Fakhri's soup. In the meantime, by the side of the street, under an awning made from an old prayer chador, she had set up a regular apothecary shop where one could buy combinations of spices or herbs for any stew or soup. When she saw the delight with which customers wolfed down her hot soup from cheap, plastic bowls, Fakhri became drunk, beside herself with a special joy, which was a feeling that even the great pleasures of the world couldn't match. The soup-eaters were all her children.

Come to think of it: What makes us fight with one another? Why can't we all get together, sit around, have some soup, and talk and laugh? Tomorrow we'll all be six feet under anyway!

At times, as she stared dumbfounded at the masses congregating at the embassy, she would round her lips and whistle softly and daydream. The dreams brought a look of happy innocence to her face. They were dreams from her youth: all the women were decent and dutiful; at dusk men would return from work with two bags full of food under their arms; at dinner time, the tablecloth would be spread on the floor; and every night, like all future nights, the bedding would be rolled out, and wives would perform their wifely duties. Thursday nights the couples would visit a shrine, have a good cry, and repent of their sins. Tomorrow won't we all be sleeping six feet under with only a length of shroud to our names?

When the young people finished their soup and turned to her to ask how much they owed, Fakhri would say, 'Nothing, just a prayer.' Thus, 'soup for a prayer' was born. This started a whole 'for a prayer' craze. After the war with Iraq broke out, 'tea for a prayer,' 'syrup for a prayer,' 'lunch for a prayer,' and even 'a shave and a shine for a prayer' became all the rage. The government was, naturally, governing 'for a prayer.'

Revolutions came one after another at that time; after several months, it was the turn of the Cultural Revolution, and once again Fakhri was sitting pretty. The university became War Central; every political group had an office or the like there. The groups would issue proclamation after proclamation, draw up strategic plans, change tactics, wait in ambush to counterstrike, and go one step forward and two steps back so many times that, after two or three years, all of them had reached a dead end. Then they were caught in gunfire, and the alleys and lanes of the city were smeared with blood and shit.

Fakhri—her breasts swinging to and fro like feedbags—would patrol up and down the area near the university, armed with a stick. She shrieked, showered people with curses, and spit. She would point to the sign on the university gate and say, 'I'm going to force them to shut down that cesspool! They have become such *important* people!'

Fakhri put her hands on her hips and stood to catch her breath. Then she wiped spittle from her mouth with the hem of her dress. She grabbed newspapers and tore them to pieces; then she wrecked the displays of books laid out on the sidewalks. She beat her chest and, raising the stick over her head, said, 'If there's one real man among you, let him come out of there, and I'll break both his legs with this stick!'

By then she had picked up a couple of lieutenants and camp followers. The Muslim kids called her 'Mother Fakhri' and idolized her; she had made a name for herself. But if not for her soup, how would she have gotten this reputation?

The Revolution was now on its way to being well established, that is, if the Communist kids and the American-backed liberals would let it. They had recruited a handful of sluts and butt boys to be their stooges, and were now charging full steam ahead against the Revolution.

It was around that time that Hasan Khanom went on one of his missions, and, after several days, came news of his death. Fakhri beat her head and her chest and lost consciousness; were it not for the strenuous efforts of the neighbors, she wouldn't have revived. In those days, it was not fashionable to rush to the bazaar to buy a couple of cookies and let all the neighbors share the happiness with the family when news of the death of a loved one came.

The crowd that gathered on the day of the funeral procession seemed endless. At first Fakhri said, 'Look at our bad luck; I suppose there is a demonstration again. How can we hold a funeral in all of this confusion?'

They explained to her that the crowd had come for the funeral, and she gave an interview immediately with the very first reporter she met on the street. All of the evening papers printed her picture. She said, 'I had a husband, and sacrificed him willingly for the Revolution!' Then they asked about the deceased's character. Fakhri spoke of his even temper and added, 'Despite his good temper, he battled all forms of indecency since he had a sense of honor.'

Then the masses shouted with one voice, 'No country has ever seen a man with more honor!'

Fakhri said, 'You should have acknowledged his worth sooner!' and made a face, showing her contempt.

At every point in the neighborhood there was a mirrored column commemorating Hasan Khanom's death, and every mosque throughout the city held memorial services for him. Sometimes Fakhri would attend several of these ceremonies in a single day, and, having long since run out of tears, she would merely stare at the crowds. Women would come by and congratulate her on her loss, saying, 'How lucky you are to be so blessed. We wish we were in your shoes.' In the mosques Mullahs would say things from their pulpits, every word of which was lost on Fakhri. They usually began with criminal America and its bloodthirsty lackeys, and then addressed the cursed Shemr and the events at Karbala.

For a time, things went well for Fakhri. Sacks of rice and tins of cooking oil would arrive at her doorstep from the local mosque. This continued until the bastard Saddam attacked. All kinds of talk, anxieties, prayers, tears, speeches, and sermons flourished again, and the whole country was in an uproar. The radio constantly broadcast the 'O, Iran' anthem, and patriotism was the watchword of the times. Night and day the television showed women holding a brazier with live charcoal in one hand while sprinkling sprigs of wild rue on it with the other. Groups of young boys emerged from the smoke, wearing green bandanas and holding *There-is-no-God-but-God* banners. They all started their journeys by passing under the Qur'an, and the crowds would break out in Karbala dirges and prayer.

Ragged lines of young people moved through the crowds on their way to the buses. As they boarded, the young men would mourn Karbala and point their upraised, clenched fists toward the front. The city was treated to scenes of smoke, mist, the dirge singer Ahangaran, green banners waving in the wind, prayers and lamentations, inflated prices, and long lines waiting for rationed foodstuffs. This was the general scene in the city.

Lump and granulated sugar, chickens, and cooking oil—everything was bought with ration coupons—even rice and cheese. Human souls and bread were plentiful, however, because bakers labored twenty-four hours a day, and women kept giving birth. People, clumped in small groups, stood in line, and, because of the constant blare of martial music from loudspeakers, they had to shout to be heard. The talk everywhere was of the retaking of a certain hill, of victory; cleansing the world of sedition, however, was a long way off.

At daybreak, women gathered in mosques to knit and sew. The neighborhood women sent tomato sauce, pickled vegetables, and sour grape juice to the front, as well as knit gloves, hats, and socks for the soldiers. The whole country was on the move. Fakhri also went to the battle lines once or twice to stitch and patch tears in soldiers' uniforms. After a while, word came from Tehran that her presence was sorely needed, and she got herself ready to depart. Again, those same girls and boys! The Communist insects had been crushed, but now the Mojahedin (dubbed Monafeqin or 'Hypocrites') were coming out in droves. But even though there were so many of them, they still brought their mothers into the streets. They had grenades and carpet cutters with them. Intense fighting would break out, and Fakhri became exhausted. They would pile the Mojahedin in buses and take them to Evin. The terrified girls, bloodied from the beatings they'd received above and below the belt, would enter through the large metal gates with yellow faces like a troop of cadavers. The continuous waves of machine-gun fire would be followed at the crack of dawn by the sharp, discordant sounds of single shots that came from the bare hills and tormented the conscience of the cursed city.

Thick crowds composed of people from every city and town gathered outside the gates of the prisons. At noon, still without permission to meet with the prisoners, they spread their kerchiefs on the ground in the shadow of a wall and, squatting, they would sit around, unhappily gnawing on dry bread. All the while their watery, bulging eyes were trained on the large iron gates of the prison.

They would bring a jug of yogurt or a live chicken with them and offer them to the guards, hoping to get them to look after their loved ones imprisoned inside. The guards made comforting promises, but group after group of prisoners would be executed, and the next day fathers and mothers would come to take possession of the bundles of clothing and the last wills and testaments of their children. In their wills the children typically wrote *give my watch to big brother; give my eyeglasses to little brother*—these were the only things among their worldly goods worth giving. Then, their shoulders heaving, the parents would go down Khavaran Road so they could tearfully recite prayers over the graves of their loved ones.

Eventually the Mojahedin sedition also died down. Fakhri wanted to return to the battle lines; but, since it was clear that they had enough volunteers for that type of work, she had to give her spot to another person.

Sitting at home was not easy for her; she had worked like mad in the streets for the Revolution. To remain useless and idle was not in her nature; so she appealed to some people from her husband's mosque, and they found something for her to do. She got a job in a small antechamber to a government office that was visited by petitioners all day long. She sat and inspected how women were made up. She would admit to the old ladies of the neighborhood, 'I can't cope with them. What's more, they have come up with lip glosses that are absolutely colorless; they only shine like lights.'

The women scratched their faces with one hand and slapped themselves with the other, saying, 'May the Lord wipe their seed from the face of the earth!'

The Americans made these glosses, and a mysterious Zionist network distributed them free of charge to women so that, instead of going to the front, our boys would chase their shapely butts and commit all kinds of sins!

Then it was the turn of nail polish, which, though it lacked color, also glistened. And then came the headscarves, which did in fact glow as if the women under them were headlamps. These lamps were forever winking and leading the youth astray.

Fakhri was responsible for inspecting the color of outer garments and determining whether they were too loose or too tight; she also examined the thinness and thickness of stockings, and was especially interested in pants, which absolutely had to reach below the ankles. She likewise looked at the heels of shoes, which could be no higher than a finger joint, which wasn't the easiest thing to estimate. Women were forced, then, to take off their shoes and give them to Fakhri. With the clammy, cloying stink of feet in her nostrils, she would draw one end of her scarf over her face and, narrowing her eyes, measure the heels against her finger.

Immodesty and disgrace could not be permitted to return to the land, and Mrs. Fakhri was ever vigilant in preventing their recurrence. America and all its bloodthirsty lackeys lay in wait twenty-four hours a day, making Fakhri's already heavy responsibilities heavier. If some woman had the gall to object to the inspections, Fakhri had a ready response: 'Is that the only answer you people can give our youth for all the blood they've lost?'

From time to time, she remembered her husband, Hasan Khanom, whose blood the anti-Revolutionaries had spilled so cruelly, and Fakhri's own blood would boil. She would strike herself with both hands and say, 'If they hadn't whipped the likes of you a couple of times, you wouldn't have come to your senses.'

The person she was speaking to, whoever it was, would quickly grasp the situation and, to avoid any misunderstanding, begin to match Fakhri sob for sob as she mourned Hasan Khanom. The person would ask her, 'Tell me about his love, his generous nature, his good works, his fine character, and his respect for the law.' Fakhri would cry harder and say, 'Stop, stop it. You're breaking my heart . . . No more!'

This was her daily routine: arguing with women who used eyeliner. Fakhri insisted, they resisted; the talk escalated into heated confrontations. Fakhri's eyes were failing her, so she moistened a corner of her handkerchief with saliva and rubbed it around their eyes. Sometimes when she brought it under the light, it would be black, but other times it wouldn't. In either case, the women attacked her, and every night Fakhri would go home out of sorts. At supper she would take her hunk of bread and toss it on the dinner cloth, saying, 'I don't want any bread I get with money for inspecting women's lipstick and measuring their heels.'

She finally went to the head of her office and said, 'Hajji, they're only young, after all; from time to time they'll want to paint their faces, wear brightly colored clothes; they've got their hopes and desires.'

The man stroked his beard, turned frankly toward Fakhri and said, 'Okay, but weren't you young once yourself? So why didn't you do such things?'

Fakhri was taken aback. She thought for a while and said, 'Times are different now, Hajji. If their shoes have an extra two centimeters, it doesn't make the Qur'an wrong!'

The head of the office turned his eyes toward heaven, directed a prayer of repentance to the Throne of God, and said, 'Sister Fakhri, you aren't getting what I'm saying. I'm a man; I know about such things. The sound women in heels make when they walk can make a man go nuts. Want me to say it more plainly? They get aroused! Should I draw you a picture? It makes them come! Now do you get it?'

Fakhri said, 'God, what can I say? You're probably right,' and she left the chief's room.

It was around this time that, out of the blue, they started saying, 'We've won. The war's over.' But the alleys were still filled with the mirrored memorials to the fallen and were given new names, the names of the martyrs of the war! People with addresses written on scraps of paper roamed the streets in vain, trying to find places. All of the squares, streets, and alleys had had their names changed; everybody was lost.

At that time Hajji Azarakhshi sent for Fakhri, saying that her presence was sorely needed. This, it seemed, was what she wanted most. She asked for one month's leave and went. The age of reconstruction had started.

Hajji Azarakhshi had several spots where he plied his trade; one was in the Gisha quarter, another was on Vali-Asr Square, and another was at Students' Park. He would station his minibus at some corner, roll up his sleeves to the elbow, and, with one foot on the curb and the other on the stairway, inspect people passing by. He was on the hunt for those they called 'Lady Gagas,' or 'Dancing Queens,' or 'Sister Sluts.' Sisters Mortezavi and Kazemi helped him in his pursuit.

Sexy girls, made up to die for, stood before the large shop windows, pointing to colorful headscarves, cheap bracelets, and open-backed high heels; they argued over whether they were made in Korea or Turkey. Occasionally they would absentmindedly laugh, slap each other on the back, and start guffawing, unaware that their momentary joy would make their headscarves slide back, revealing black or brown forelocks with blond highlights or curls. Hajji Azarakhshi would swoop down on them like an eagle. They were laughing, weren't they?

Cries of terror rubbed the girls' delicate throats raw. Grabbing the girls by their lapels, the sisters would drag them along the ground to the minibus, and, on the way, pinch them so hard relatives both living and dead learned of it. The prisoners would get on the bus, but not before Hajji Azarakhshi had spit in their faces.

Thick crowds would gather by the sidewalk. Once the minibus was full, it drove off in triumph. Triangular green flags hanging from the half-open windows of the bus fluttered in the wind, while throngs of people on the sidewalk, like bloated corpses, remained motionless, mute, their eyes bulging from their sockets as they hovered in the air. They were victorious in every war.

At times the girls would resist. Fakhri, who was more of a bruiser than the other two women, would bring their arms up from behind their backs, and the girls, gasping for breath, would submit. That was the cue for Sisters Mortezavi and Kazemi to begin the reeducation process. Once Sister Mortezavi pinched the face, breasts, and throat of a girl so brutally that Fakhri was forced to yell, 'These are prisoners, you infidel! You're practically killing some poor person's child!'

Sister Mortezavi got offended and said to Hajji Azarakhshi, 'If we don't make them listen to reason today, tomorrow they'll become whores and lead our young men astray.'

'To hell with our young men!' shouted Fakhri. 'We can't go around killing the girls just because the boys might be led astray!'

Fakhri continued going out with them but stopped after one week. At night when she went to sleep, the terrified looks on the faces of the girls stayed with her until morning. It was as if she were going through a tunnel lined with the skulls of the dead and echoing with cries of horror—it was horrible. No, never again would she go on the minibus.

A rumor spread among the other women that Sister Fakhri was having doubts and needed reassurance. They surrounded her and said, 'These kids are a bunch of Communists! Do you know what that means?'

The bad thing about Communists is this: to them there's no difference between 'mine' and 'yours.' When they go to sleep at night, they take off their clothes and pile them in a corner.

When they get up in the morning, they go to the pile and put on whatever comes to hand; everything from underwear to socks belongs to the group. It's the same with their tooth-brushes and drinking cups; that's why their group hideouts are infected with scabies and syphilis.

Next came the satellite dishes. When you looked at Tehran from above, you saw roofs full of things looking like pot lids. The black-and-white screens of televisions became full of vibrant, jubilant colors. On the outskirts of the city some sold tickets to people without satellites so they could come and watch. *Baywatch* cost 500 tumans. Because private homes couldn't accommodate all the customers, long lines formed an hour before the series started. The lines stretched from deep within the alleyways to the main streets, where luxury vehicles passed by, taking their high-ranking passengers to offices and ministries. The *Baywatch* viewers were the very ones who, just ten or twelve years before, had been killing these passengers or driving them into exile. These high-ranking officers, however, reemerged like things that hatch from the black eggs deposited in the moist rims of sewer openings and, in time, turn into full-size, well-nourished cockroaches.

14

Fattah rang the bell again, and, when the door silently opened a crack, he said, 'Hello, madam, is Mirza in?'

The two parts of the door brushed against each other but didn't close, and Khanjan ran back to her room to put on her chador. From behind the door she raised her voice and said, 'Please, come in.'

Fattah stepped into the hallway and closed the door behind him. The half-lit hall, with the floor of loose bricks forever wetted down and swept, and its quiet air of spirituality, always made Fattah feel bolder and put him in a good mood. Today, of course, he was immeasurably sad.

Khanjan pointed in the direction of the yard and said, 'He's down there.'

Fattah turned his head toward the plaster wall, looked down, and, with affected innocence, said, 'I'm disturbing you!'

Now totally absolved of any possible offence, he followed the base of the wall and entered the yard.

Khanjan went back inside. She knew him; he was one of Mirza's devotees, but she didn't like him. He would visit Mirza from time to time, sit by his floor cushion for a few minutes, then go. He earned a good living and was one of those people who supplied Mirza with cash. Otherwise, where would Mirza get the money to help all the penniless people?

Fattah went down the steps to the basement. At first he couldn't see anything in front of him because it was so dark. He even imagined Mirza was not there, but light from the outside shone on one end of a carpet, revealing a pair of slippers with worn soles and curled-up toes. He looked again and saw the outline of Mirza, who had his head in a book. As he stood there waiting, Mirza raised his head; now his face was completely bathed in light, and the darkness—at least this is what Fattah thought—had receded. He greeted the old man and stood waiting by the carpet.

Mirza closed the book and said, 'Is that you, Fattah? Well, what do you know!'

Fattah bowed slightly, took his shoes off, and came forward, saying, 'At your service, sir!'

He knelt down beside the carpet and tried to kiss Mirza's hand, but he put it behind his back. Fattah bent down and touched his forehead to Mirza's shoulder; Mirza caressed his head, and Fattah bit his lip, about to cry.

Both remained motionless and quiet for a moment; Fattah's fleshy hands rested on his knees as he kept his eyes on the floor. Coming to Mirza gave Fattah strength; in the whole world he was the one person to whom Fattah could open his heart—he was like a father. Yes, a real father! And this was the thing that gave him a sense of bliss and security; in this city he possessed something unique: a father!

Mirza said, 'How unexpected! What made you come this way?'

Fattah said, 'No one is more devoted to you, sir. Pray for me.'

Looking at him, Mirza nodded and said, 'May God grant you success in the end!'

Fattah said, 'Very kind of you, sir. A problem's come up.'

Mirza nodded again. Fattah raised his head and looked at Mirza, who was still nodding. Fattah said, 'Tell me something, sir, that will bolster my heart!'

There was a hint of darkness in the depths of the old man's bright look, but he said, 'It'll work out!'

Fattah stirred and, overcome with joy, said, 'I can't thank you enough, sir. Truly!'

Mirza slowly closed his eyes and nodded again. Fattah began to sob like a little boy and tried to kiss Mirza's hand once more. As he did so he said, 'Sir, I want to become a real man, repent, get a wife, have a family, go on pilgrimages. All of it!'

A lump in his throat kept him from saying more, but a moment later, his voice hoarse, he said, 'From now on, I'm going to say my prayers, observe the difference between what's lawful and what's not, never . . . never offend people's honor.'

When he got to this point, he began blubbering again. He covered his eyes with his hand for a moment and his shoulders quaked; then, silent again, he put his hand in his pocket—looking for his handkerchief—and began to cry silently.

Mirza merely looked at him. His head still resting on his shoulder, Fattah took out his handkerchief and rubbed his eyes. He said, 'Pray for me, sir!'

With his head still on the old man's shoulder, he kept sobbing. He took out a wad of bills and put it under the old man's cushion. Then he got up on his knees and said, 'At least let me kiss your hand, sir.'

Mirza said, 'It's not necessary.'

Then he was silent again. Fattah blew his nose a few times and said, 'Do I have permission to go, sir?'

Mirza reached behind him and picked up a knotted handkerchief. He opened it, picked out a piece of rock candy, and put it in Fattah's hand. Fattah kissed the candy, touched it to his eyelids, then rose to his feet.

Before Fattah left, the lump in his throat broke again. Mirza said, 'Make sure your intentions are good: everything is in His hands!'

Fattah nodded eagerly, like a child; these, it seems, were exactly the words he had wanted to hear. He laid his shoes out, put them on, and went up the stairs. The yard was bathed in midday sunshine; he felt relieved.

Khanjan and Batul were busy talking in the hallway. When they heard Fattah coming, they gathered their chadors and turned their backs. Fattah once again clung to the wall, keeping his head down as his fat feet propelled him toward the door. There he said goodbye and left.

Khanjan said, 'He's gone . . . now you go.'

Batul had a lot of faith in Mirza's healing powers, even though Dr. Candy had cured her back pain. She remembered going early one day to Dr. Candy's office, which was somewhere uptown, and waiting two or three hours to see him. Dr. Candy, wearing a white coat and sporting a white beard, put a piece of rock candy the size of a chick pea in Batul's palm and waved his hand in the air near her back. Then he said, 'Now go!'

Batul dissolved the candy in water, and each day swallowed a spoonful of the mixture. Before a week had gone by, her back pain was gone. People came to Dr. Candy's office on crutches or with their arms in splints; they even brought in a man on a ladder. Others arrived on stretchers, bandaged and groaning, or attached to serum drips. They brought old men and women in large wicker baskets, and the doctor cured them; he treated everyone, his hands were so gifted. Batul almost died when she saw a person with skin hanging from his face and neck; he had been pulled from a fire and brought straight to Dr. Candy.

Batul went from the yard to the basement. In the luminous emptiness, which at first seemed dark, she hadn't reached the bottom of the steps when she greeted Mirza and said, 'Sir, I've come again to request something from you!'

More radiant than he had ever been, Mirza said with a laugh, 'What's happened now?'

Batul hesitated, then said, 'It's for a reputable person again.'

As though beset by worry, Mirza sighed and said, 'Come and sit down.'

Batul came forward and sat by the cushion. Mirza moved his jaws and looked hard at the woman; then he said, 'How much do you want?'

Batul said, 'It's for the same woman you graciously helped a few weeks back when her daughter had an operation. The woman wants her daughter to get married, but she's got absolutely nothing to her name!'

Batul said this as if the heartbreak were her own.

Mirza nodded. He reached under the cushion for the same bills Fattah had put there and pulled them out. He gave the money to Batul, saying, 'May God grant success to all people in the end!'

Batul made a benediction and said to Mirza, 'You are my master, sir!'

Mirza nodded, and Batul, never turning her back on him, groped her way to the foot of the stairs. Then she said, 'Sir, if we didn't have you . . .'

Mirza, with an ancient and remote calm, nodded, and, from a place of deep inner serenity, said, 'Give thanks to God!'

15

When Mostafa came home that night, he was in absolutely no mood to talk; as soon as he finished dinner, he went straight to bed. The next morning, trying to get him to say something, Khanjan spoke of the cold, the high rent on the house, and the neighbor boy's addiction, but Mostafa refused to open his mouth. Khanjan knew what was eating him, and, getting right to the heart of the matter, said, 'There's no shortage of girls. You should be thankful you're in good health, and you've got an honest job that lets you put food on the table!'

Mostafa finally said, 'Why don't you pay them a little visit and get them to tell you what's holding up the decision? What the hell's wrong with them, anyway?'

Khanjan leaned in close to her son and said, 'What for? If you ask me, they're just trying to jack up the price of the goods!' Then she drew back and, with a knowing look on her face, repeated, 'There's no shortage of girls out there!'

'No shortage, yes,' agreed Mostafa. 'But of the thousands of girls you have in mind for me, it's this one that I want. Only this one!'

Then he put on his jacket and left the room. He wheeled his motorcycle from the hallway, got on, and drove off.

He had taken out the frustration he felt on that poor girl by pounding her head into the wall that day. Her screams reached the ward office. According to Keramat, if she received another beating like that, she'd start talking.

Mostafa managed to weave his way through the traffic, but there were times it became so snarled he had to bring the motorcycle onto the sidewalk and drive there until the street cleared. People everywhere, shrieking all the time—it was as if haste and futility were the main core of their existence.

The sky over the city had no horizon; there was probably some covering, some bronze dome that kept the clean, bright, and beautiful world, which had to exist above the city, from being contaminated by the rank odors and tortured sounds.

The leaden atmosphere, the congestion, and the misery seemed to seep into people and, unavoidably, to become more noxious. It was a satanic city, a city feuding with the Lord; its bustling, choked thoroughfares must be like the corridors of hell.

Although Mostafa had left home an hour before, it was only at this point he noticed that, instead of going to the office, he was cruising around Shahrzad's house. He stopped by a newspaper kiosk and bought a couple of cigarettes. He parked his motorcycle on the side of the street, lit a cigarette, and leaned against a tree. From here he could see the door to her house on the alley. Then he looked at his watch; it was around the time she usually left.

He lit another cigarette. The door remained closed; then he looked at his watch again and spit. A relatively forceful gust of wind blowing along the ground suddenly caused dirt and bits of paper to whip up and whirl about. Mostafa looked at the sky; you couldn't rely on the weather—you couldn't rely on anything in this city. It had been on the verge of rain for two days.

Finally Shahrzad emerged from the house. Mostafa lifted the kickstand with his foot, got on the motorcycle, started it, and drove into the alley. Shahrzad turned, and Mostafa stopped.

'Hop on, and let's go!'

He indicated where she should sit with his eyes. Without a word, Shahrzad lifted the hem of her chador, put her left leg over the seat, and wrapped her arms around Mostafa. Then they were off.

They traveled down streets and passed squares; sometimes a flyover, bulging from the ground like a buried corpse, would join parts of a road that another road had divided.

Their journey took them to Vali-Asr Square, where the plane trees provided cool shade all spring and summer; but on this fall morning their bare, dry branches seemed to gesture threateningly toward heaven. When they reached a relatively open spot, the motorcycle began to fly, causing the fetid air to beat harder against their faces and tears to flow from their eyes.

Shahrzad had no choice but to press her breasts against Mostafa's back, close her eyes, and bury her head between his shoulders. From some mysterious source she suddenly felt a gentle warmth flow into her body—the momentary stirring! But the cool autumn air relaxed her, soothed her fever, and, at once, a kind of pure equanimity replaced the strange feeling.

A soft breeze caressed the city, the tree branches shook, and a simple, cheap happiness was to be had. At the little market in Tajrish Square they were met by the perfume of spices and the sheen of white prayer shawls with floral prints, rank smells and scurrying feet, modest shop windows lit with fluorescent lights, and displays of dried fruits, barberries, and dates. Laid out also were bolts of fabric—hand-stamped cloth, thick cotton, velvet, and silks—in every color; uneven sidewalks, narrow lanes, peddlers shouting, and then the dome and finials of the Imamzadeh Saleh Shrine came into view. They entered the yard, gave their shoes to a shoe-keeper and proceeded to the metal grate around the sepulcher; it was there that Shahrzad sobbed loudly.

First Darband Street, then the square; he chained the motorcycle to a tree, and they strolled, keeping close to the walls. The sky was clear and blue again, but that didn't diminish their anguish. They walked for hours, hearing only the sound of each other's breathing. They reached a steep incline, then a row of teahouses. Yellow leaves under their feet, the sounds of the stream in their ears, and everything in a perfect, white halo that had a physical substance and seemed to radiate from the rocks. Now they were together, alone, silent, as if they had nothing to say. Once or twice Mostafa dared to take the girl's hand. Shahrzad was conscious of what he was doing; she didn't object; a kind of mild desire even issued from her fingers and passed into Mostafa's body.

She was aware of what she was doing, and, on that fall morning, they were suddenly, immoderately sad. It seemed they were having a premonition that something bad was about to happen, and knew how brief these moments were. Mostafa began to hum, and Shahrzad's eyes became moist.

Then Mostafa said, 'You have nothing to say?'

Shahrzad merely looked at him through teary eyes.

'You know many of my friends went to the front and died in the war; but I survived, and now I want to get married! I want to live!'

He said this in a determined and serious way, tinged with a little pride, that suggested this was the final battle of his life. The girl looked at the stream as they both stood there.

Shahrzad asked, 'Live?'

As if frightened by the unpleasant echo of the word, she said again, 'Live?'

This time her voice was hoarse, but she turned and looked directly at Mostafa, who, apparently embarrassed, looked down and said, 'Yeah, well! What's wrong with us?'

Shahrzad said under her breath, 'Us?'

Then she was silent. Everywhere she looked seemed misty; at times a tear dripped from the corner of her eye; then her vision cleared for a few moments, only to cloud over again.

They kept walking until they saw an out-of-the-way teahouse and realized they couldn't go any further. It was a lonely place with the shadowy figure of a *kamancheh*-player, whose only audience was a solitary man smoking a water pipe in a corner.

As was the case every fall, they had collected the wooden settees from the banks of the stream and brought them inside the teahouse. But for the faint flame under the large brass samovar on the cement counter, it was dark inside. The fragrance of tea and the odor of stagnation rose on the steam coming from the samovar and drifted around under the low ceiling. The cherry-red Turkmen carpets, which covered the short legs of the settees, seemed to hover, weightless, over the ground, and a kind of inertia and illusion made the dark corners of the teahouse stretch toward unseen spaces.

They sat; shadows of the bare branches could be seen through the teahouse's filmy windows. Shahrzad leaned her elbow on the carpet and bent her head toward her shoulder.

'This doctor won't give up,' she said. 'My mother is torn now, but he'll win her over in the end!'

Mostafa pounded his fist on the carpet and said, 'I won't let that happen! I won't; you'll see!'

Shahrzad looked at the thick smoke from the man's water pipe. She took another look, as though it was her world the smoke was concealing.

A dull light shone down from the grimy ceiling of the teahouse. Shahrzad said, 'He won't give up!'

This signaled a kind of finality, as if the next thing out of her mouth would be: *I'm going to take poison!*

Mostafa, gathering his thoughts, hesitated before he spoke. He took two short breaths before inhaling fully, as if air was in short supply. Then he said, 'We'll run away!'

A waiter, who was pouring tea, stopped to look at them. What did they know about each other? About life? Everything was shrouded in darkness.

With a feeling of pure desperation, Shahrzad said, 'There's no other way, you mean?'

Mostafa absentmindedly moved his jaw and raised his chin. The waiter put the tea glasses in front of them and went back behind the counter.

'He's rich, a doctor with lots of muscle behind him!' Shahrzad said.

'I don't care who he is!'

Yes, those people with a lot of power and pull. Was it possible for Mostafa to be one of them, so he wouldn't have to suffer so, have to endure such misery?

Shahrzad said, 'They'll find us wherever we go!'

Then that man, the man with the muscle, would take possession of Shahrzad. Mostafa looked at her. He lowered his voice and said, 'I'll kill him!'

In a way that perhaps only she could hear, Shahrzad said, 'No.'

Then she looked down and unfolded a napkin she had crumpled in her fist; for a long time she stared at it as if it were completely unfamiliar. Then she crumpled it again, threw it on the carpet and started to cry. Mostafa was also on the verge of tears, which was why he rose and went to the window. On the bank of the stream two puppies were nuzzling each other with their wet snouts and growling. He looked at the puppies, then he wiped the steam from the window with his sleeve, and suddenly they could be seen by everyone.

He dropped Shahrzad off at the head of the alley that evening and said, 'I'll pick you up and take you with me. We'll run away, get away from these people, go to a place where no one will find us!'

All she said was, 'How?'

Mostafa nodded and said, 'Soon, you'll see!'

Mostafa gunned the engine and looked straight ahead. He took a deep breath and peered at the sky. Shahrzad turned without saying goodbye and went to the sidewalk. Mostafa watched her go for a few moments and, as if all the cares in the world were on his shoulders, shook his head sadly, turned the motorcycle around, stepped on the gas, and left.

16

There are occasions when the presence of a father and mother is essential. A trip, sickness, or even death cannot excuse their absence. Mothers, of course, attend these occasions more often than fathers, who arrive late or never come. Here, on that fall morning, was Fattah, on his way to his bride's home to fix the date of the wedding. The feeling of being without a father was now more wearying than at any other time in his life; it felt like a heavy growth pressing down on his chest.

One of the unknowns in the city was why some boys looked more like their paternal uncles or one of the football stars, or even like the models in newspaper advertisements, than their fathers! Walking along the street, Fattah saw sons with their fathers and would study them closely, wanting to dispel his cynicism. The result was mostly regrettable; many of the fathers were suspect. Their sons resembled the actors in television serials more than they did the men they called 'father.'

Lost in these thoughts, Fattah suddenly found himself standing in Shahrzad's yard. He walked forward and, in no mood for niceties, got straight to the point.

'Don't be grumpy with me. For people like us, given our work and the situation, we've never begged any girl for her hand; girls come to us on their own two feet.'

His look, the way he moved his hands, in fact, everything about him, spoke of money and power. This was not lost on an experienced woman like Mehri. So she had no choice, it seemed, but to agree with what he said. She nodded and said, 'Yes, of course!'

Fattah kept staring at her, and Mehri repeated, 'Yes!'

She felt a chill inside, and, perhaps to compensate for the feeling, she blurted out, 'Yes, Doctor, well, those kinds of girls, but my daughter . . .'

She was quiet. They looked at each other; the look in Fattah's eyes had a particular meaning. He nodded slowly and, with a knowing smile, said, 'They're all cut from the same cloth, dear lady! You can be sure of that. These girls!'

With a disparaging gesture, he threw his hands behind his head. The muscles in Mehri's face tightened. She lifted her head and looked at the man; all at once her eyes glistened with tears. Fattah became alarmed and said, 'But Shahrzad is different. I know . . . I know that for a fact!'

Tears streamed down Mehri's face. Fattah, with unaccustomed sympathy, said, 'But I want your daughter!'

Mehri believed him; she was able to tell when people were lying. The man's look was empty of any sordidness; it was, rather, freighted with a peculiar tragedy.

The woman looked at him in a way that was, of course, vacant and cold. He had fallen in love, but why didn't anybody take him seriously? Couldn't he, at least, be able to tell the truth once in his life? Before this time, women had been merely a warm opening; this was the way he viewed all women. Of course, mothers were different; they were a breed apart, different from women. But now he suddenly realized that the two were the same. Now all he craved was her; the only thing he wanted was to be with her, just to look at her or . . . run his hand through her hair, slowly, in a way that wouldn't alarm her; caress her, breathe in her scent—that's all! But he was afraid; he feared hearing her say 'no,' and, due to the intensity of that fear, he blurted out, 'After all, I have connections to certain places, but it's not necessary to tell you about that. Suffice it to say, any girl who sets foot in my home will rule like an empress, an empress, dear lady! No door is closed to people like us in this country!'

He spoke the last sentence with such pride it alarmed Mehri. So he was threatening her now. Although the childish obstinacy in his tone was evident, once again it made Mehri's blood run cold. She slowly managed to say, 'Isn't happiness all a mother wants for her child?'

Taking advantage of this implicit point of agreement, Fattah said, 'That's right! That's exactly what I'm saying!' Then he cautioned her, 'Consider the happiness of your daughter!' and wagged his finger at her.

Mehri examined her intended son-in-law out of the corner of her eye. His fleshy, unwrinkled face offered no attractions, but his lips and nose were regular, and he had a mole on his right cheek. He appeared withdrawn; but it seemed there was a particular air about him, slightly bitter and stringent, that stopped people from liking him. So she said, 'Is it possible to force her into a match that she doesn't want?'

'Who?' asked Fattah.

Mehri said, 'Shahrzad . . . I'm talking about Shahrzad!'

She laughed carelessly and intimately. Fattah banged his chest with his hand and said, 'Leave that to me!'

He felt triumphant; his double chin glowed, as did the look in his eyes, and he giggled so softly and bewitchingly, Mehri's body was paralyzed by a vague, womanly feeling.

Here was a man with money and power—then why the objections?

Fattah didn't come in, and, naturally, Mehri didn't insist; but she thought even if a stranger were to knock on her door and come in, shouldn't a person serve him at least a glass of unsweetened tea? So Mehri said, 'I swear on Shahrzad's soul, it pains me to see you standing there. Let's go inside, at least.'

Fattah declined her invitation with a wave of his hand. He remained in the yard with one foot resting on the edge of the cement font. He had said his piece, and now he wanted to go; but then he said, 'I'll take her to the registry office and record the marriage agreement. I won't hold a celebration of our marriage; instead, I'll put down a substantial home on the agreement, lock stock and barrel!'

He had made his final point; Mehri was dazed. Fattah repeated, 'A substantial home!'

Then he took a document from his pocket and held it out to Mehri. 'Keep this with you and, when it's time to go to the registry, I'll put it in her name.'

Mehri looked at the document with its lead seal and strip of green ribbon on the end. It seemed to Mehri that this paper, with the short cotton ribbon swinging, indifferently, from one end, constituted her darling daughter's entire life. Fattah said, 'Take it! It's a real house!'

Mehri's hand didn't move, and she lacked the will to speak. She looked down at the stranger's waxed, shiny shoes.

Finally Fattah, his words seemingly blurted out, said, 'I mean, she's already seen it.'

Mehri suddenly looked up and, doubting that she had heard correctly, hesitant and uncertain, asked, 'Who's already seen the house?'

Her voice was shaking, but Fattah, ignoring her, said, 'The day after tomorrow, ten o'clock in the morning, I'll come by, and we'll go to the registry. I know the notary, of course.'

Mehri mumbled slowly, 'At least allow—'

Fattah interrupted her. 'My patience is at an end, dear lady! Understand?'

He turned, put the document on the edge of the font, and stood with his back to the woman. His manly grandeur, it seemed, was manifest even from behind. Mehri was tongue-tied, but, her eyes moist, she managed to say, 'When a boy and a girl are close in age, they'll get along better; she has no father to . . .'

Fattah turned and, in a dreary tone said, 'I too have no father!'

Mehri said sympathetically, 'But you . . . you don't need one anymore because you're the age of a father!'

Fattah narrowed his eyes, and, with an unexpected sordidness, said, 'Two birds with one stone: I'll be both husband and father to her!'

Through half-closed eyes, he examined the woman with that lustful look of his and smirked. Then, with his body that, like all middle-aged men, had gone flabby around the waist, behind, and stomach, but still wanted to appear young, he turned on one foot and, with feigned deftness, went to the door. He would need to wear a disguise from now on.

Yielding to her ambivalent feelings, Mehri raised her voice and said futilely, 'Tea's ready; just have a glass of unsweetened tea.'

Fattah turned his back on her, raised his hand in a gesture of thanks, and opened the front door. Mehri went to him, but the man was already through the door. The woman muttered, 'God be with you.'

Before she closed the door, she noticed two women in the house across the street, looking at her through a crack in their curtains.

17

Mostafa had scarcely gotten home when the telephone rang. On that early evening in the fall, the sound was an unexpected occurrence, which, like any sudden noise, echoed peculiarly, filling their quiet home with apprehension and misgiving. It seemed as if somebody said, *This telephone call is for you.* So he picked up the receiver. Shahrzad was at the other end; this was the first time she had called. Confident that it wasn't one of her old friends, Khanjan returned to kitchen. Mostafa was shocked, and, panting as though he had run a long race, said, 'Has something happened?'

'It's finished,' said Shahrzad.

He had trouble hearing her; her voice was faint, but a particular sort of hopelessness in her tone was unmistakable, as well as resignation.

'What's finished?' asked Mostafa.

'The doctor is coming the day after tomorrow to clinch the deal.'

Her voice was icy; Mostafa, not understanding, paused. Then he asked, 'Meaning . . .?'

Shahrzad sighed and, as though declaring an end to things, said, 'Meaning he's taking me to the register office!'

So that was the situation! Mostafa reacted immediately. 'He's making a fucking mistake!'

That not being enough, he added, 'I'll kill him!'

He spoke through clenched teeth, with so much hatred that the receiver shook in his hand. There was silence on the other end of the line. Mostafa balled his other hand into a fist and raised it in the air. His entire body shaking, he angrily slammed the receiver down on the cradle. Without taking his hand from the receiver, he stood there motionless.

Thoughts came into his head, none clear, rolling one on top of another. A wave of dizziness broke over him, and eventually some force within made him whirl and rave like a madman. He went on like this for quite a while; then, before the tremors and mental turmoil robbed him of his faculties, the telephone rang again.

The muscles in his face vibrated in harmony with the metallic ringing, and he didn't have the nerve to answer it. From the kitchen Khanjan asked, 'Where are you? Why don't you pick up?'

Mostafa picked up the receiver.

'Why did you hang up?'

Mostafa had no answer. He put on his clothes, wheeled his motorcycle from the hall to the alley, closed the door, and left.

From the house to work wasn't a short distance, but Mostafa was blind to the cars, the people, and the red lights along the way. Crazed and only half aware of what was happening, he made the motorcycle fly and got there in half an hour. He hurried to the cell where Manizheh was being held in solitary confinement. Mostafa stood over the poor girl, who was in a state between sleep and wakefulness, lying in a corner.

'Were a donkey to receive such beatings, it would have confessed,' said Mostafa, and then he kicked her viciously in the groin. The poor little thing rolled into a ball, then she opened her eyes and showed him her profile. She wasn't feeling right, but managed to look at Mostafa with contempt.

Several minutes later, when Mostafa returned the key to the guard, he was a totally different man. He gave him a mischievous look and said, 'She finally talked!'

The guard got halfway out of his chair and said, 'Really? You swear?'

Mostafa nodded his head in triumph, declaring, 'Just when everyone had almost given up hope!'

He nodded again, and the guard couldn't contain himself. He rushed forward and gave Mostafa several congratulatory pats on the arm; naturally, he viewed the victory as partly his. Mostafa marched from the wing in triumph.

As he walked to Keramat's office, he kept his hands in his pockets. After what seemed like eons, he felt perfectly at peace, and he started to whistle. What was it he was whistling? Something like a love song, perhaps?

The door to Keramat's office was locked, and Mostafa, his fist still on the handle, turned toward the guard watching him. Keramat had left the prison an hour ago. Mostafa once again twisted the handle and murmured, 'I've got to talk to him!'

Mostafa entered the guardroom. It was early evening, a time when Mostafa was usually at home. At this time of the day the prison seemed exceptionally quiet and empty to him. 'I'll have to call him!' he said, feeling helpless.

The guard pointed to the telephone. Mostafa dialed the number, rounded his lips again, and whistled. He was so excited that as soon as Keramat answered, Mostafa said, 'Keramat, sir, she finally gave in.'

'Who?' asked Keramat.

'That subject of mine!'

As he said this, he nodded his head in confirmation as if Keramat were standing in front of him or could see him.

'Bravo!' said Keramat. Then he asked, 'What did she say?'

'She gave me her name, address . . . everything.'

Keramat said, 'What are you waiting for, then? Send in the boys . . . no, I'll tell them myself. Now, out with her name and address!'

Mostafa said, 'Write this down: her name is Shahrzad Bakhtiari!'

'Tell me her address!'

'Lorzadeh Alley, across from the Ziba Baths, house number fourteen. The girl's no more than nineteen. There's only herself and her mother in the house.'

Keramat said, 'Very good. Bye, now!'

Mostafa also said goodbye, and, as he put the receiver down, that unique feeling of perfect peace came over him again. He tried whistling, but couldn't remember a tune. He paused for a bit, shook his head energetically, but it didn't help; everything, it seemed, had sunk into darkness once more.

18

The windowpanes shook suddenly, and a cold, sustained rush of air made everything solid or movable seem to float. Then came the sound of stomping feet. Terrified, Mehri raised her head; at that point two men toting guns dropped down from the wall. Mehri lost her voice, then her consciousness.

Before Shahrzad could get to the yard, the door to the house opened, and three armed men entered. Shahrzad stepped back; all the men were screaming, making her completely unable to move. One of them grabbed Shahrzad's arms from behind and brought them up to her shoulders; prolonged pain trapped the air in her lungs. At the same time, another man pried her mouth open and yelled, 'Do you have cyanide? Do you have cyanide?'

He stuck his finger into her mouth and felt under her tongue and along her jaw. Finally he pushed her to the ground. Shahrzad rubbed her shoulders and started to cough. She felt a constant hammering in her skull, which made her head feel like it was as big as the entire yard.

They searched the whole house, rummaging through the bedding, pulling clothing from drawers and armoires—

basically, everything that was stored in those two small rooms was thrown into the yard. They even examined tins of spices in the kitchen, which were of no use to them. What was the thing they kept insisting she had hidden in the house? Shahrzad had no idea.

The alley was teeming with officers, and the windows of the neighbors' homes were filled with fleeting shadows. Corners of curtains were folded back, and the curious eyes of women were trained on the empty spaces where familiar objects had been. The alley, which during the day was usually filled with the shouts of the children and the racket made by peddlers, was now a mute, motionless world soon to make way for the quick steps, shouted commands, and pandemonium of the assault team. Things that could once be seen suddenly disappeared, leaving only the assaulters.

They got in the car; she was placed in the backseat with one of them on either side of her. They put her head in a sack and jammed it into the space between the two front seats. Her back was hunched over, and her slim shoulders trembled slightly like a dying sparrow's wings.

Half dead, Mehri dragged herself to the gate as the car sped off. Her walk was labored, and her voice failed her.

It was evening, and the alley was still dead. The car turned into the street.

The street was in an uproar, but they, of course, went speeding along. There were the sounds of sudden braking, ear-piercing honking, vile curses. Occasionally they stopped at a red light, and Shahrzad heard footsteps and the hubbub of the crowd; people were on their way home, with food under their arms or not, well intentioned or otherwise. Naturally they were content with whatever God willed; everything was in His hands, even a leaf dropping from a tree—it was all down to fate.

She heard the rush of water, which was most probably flowing in a roadside channel; suddenly she was thirsty. She sensed that the car had stopped, and one of them said, 'Shit!'

The car noisily shifted gears and lurched forward. She felt thirsty again, and her mouth was so dry her tongue couldn't move. The dizziness returned, and she felt they were going down a steep incline. Her eyes burned as they never had before, and she kept them shut as tightly as possible. Before that, everything was pitch dark, but suddenly a thin vein of bright blue light appeared.

Yes, everything was clear, the incident at the house so explicit. Entertaining any dreams now seemed pointless; but, from deep within, a great force had welled up, fanning her imagination and diminishing the intensity of what had just happened. She thought to herself, 'I may have set foot in another world!'

She felt cold and tried to move her hands; but she realized the men were clutching them from behind. With this reminder, a terrible pain suddenly shot through her shoulders.

Certain things looked familiar, but she didn't know their names; perhaps she'd come to know them in a nightmare, in which she was walking stark naked in the muck on the cold streets. Strangely, no one noticed her, but pain and shame had enveloped her entire body like a sticky, agonizing film. Then one of them said, 'Don't move!'

She didn't move; there were only the beginnings of a painful unconsciousness. But she wanted to stay conscious; this gave her hope. She declared, 'I'm still alive,' and felt exhilarated.

Now she was on another route, and it seemed as though she had joined a procession of mourners walking in the shade of plane trees on an endless street. There were fumes from burning wild rue, Moharram banners, and young men beating themselves with chains and banging cymbals.

A hand pressed down on her head. She couldn't move, and felt she was suffocating; she showed her agitation with a couple of dry heaves each time she heard swearing. They still hadn't arrived, and never had Shahrzad thought the road to hell would be this long.

The car stopped, the driver opened the window, and said in triumph, 'This is us!'

So they had arrived; she heard the creaking of hinges and the double iron gates moved, disturbing the air. This was the gate to hell—but did hell have a gate?

The large gate was now open, and the car entered the Evin compound. Yes, they had finally reached their destination, which the driver announced in a loud voice.

Yelling! This was basic to who they were; they were forever shouting. It was as if no one would notice them unless they were yelling.

The back doors of the car opened, and the two agents stepped out, yanking Shahrzad's arms from opposite directions. She emitted a gut-wrenching shriek, which was the last sound they heard from her.

They entered the hallway.

'You brought her?'

It was Mostafa's voice. They all stood around, and Mostafa reached out and pulled the sack from her head. For some reason it suddenly occurred to him that this was exactly what a groom does when he lifts the veil from his bride's face. Astonished, Shahrzad looked at him silently for a long time; he couldn't read anything in her eyes. Then Mostafa turned his head and said, 'Take her to cell number seven.'

This was not the first time such a thing had happened. Another interrogator had fallen in love with his neighbor's daughter, and, having been rejected, had her arrested on some pretext and put in prison. They brought the girl to his room every day, and, before starting the interrogation, he made her stand blindfold in front of him for hours as he stared at her. The poor girl never found out the real reason for her imprisonment, nor did she ever learn her interrogator's identity. A year later the interrogator was unexpectedly transferred to another prison, but the unfortunate girl was left behind with a record full of strange and contradictory confessions. Mostafa didn't know what eventually happened to the girl; he had never seen the interrogator, either. This was one of the amazing tales the guards whispered to one another during their off-duty hours.

They shoved Shahrzad into the cell and closed the door behind her. She lay in a peculiar state of numbness for a time; then she sat up. She was alone.

She didn't know where she was or why she was there; everything had happened so quickly. High above her a dim lamp shone in the middle of the black ceiling. A crumpled black blanket lay nearby and, farther away, was the gaping, fetid opening of the toilet—that was all. Of course, near the ceiling there was a window revealing small patches of sky.

In the quiet Shahrzad kept staring at the sky, and suddenly asked herself why she hadn't looked at it before.

She heard what seemed to be familiar footsteps; a key turned in the lock, the door opened, and Shahrzad looked up to see Mostafa.

Mostafa closed the door behind him, approached Shahrzad, knelt before her, and took her head in his arms. She remained motionless, not even breathing.

Stricken with fear, Mostafa pulled away from Shahrzad and, his face close to hers, looked her straight in the eye; she seemed lifeless. The fright and jostling had sapped her strength, and her ashen eyes were full of a peculiar terror. She turned her head automatically toward the window.

'Look at me!' commanded Mostafa.

His peremptory tone was clearly one born of habit.

Shahrzad looked at him, then asked, 'Where is this place?'

It was a rebuke rather than a question.

Mostafa lowered his head and said, 'Don't be afraid. I couldn't think of any other solution. Tomorrow morning, both of us are going to be free. We'll go someplace far away where no one can reach us.'

He stared automatically at the patch of sky in the window.

Shahrzad said, 'There's no such place.'

Then she shook her shoulders visibly; she seemed to be trying to brush something from them. There was nothing there, of course, but she shook them again, this time even touching them with her hand. After a while she brought her hand down.

Mostafa nodded absently; both of them seemed to be thinking the same thought at that moment, and this same thought was so dubious and dark their only reaction was fear. Despite that, Mostafa insisted, 'There is! You'll see!'

Maybe it did exist, and they would leave early the next morning, with Shahrzad on the back of his motorcycle. Where to? Perhaps the north—yes, the north, where there was plenty of work. Now was the time to pick oranges; after that would come the rice harvest, then tea. He'd be paid by the day and bring home some bread at night when Shahrzad would spread the dinner cloth. He smiled and, though only the darkness of the cell was around him, he held all the colors of the world in his mind. How far away was that dream, after all?

As though she had no tongue, Shahrzad listened to him in silence; she was far from his dreams, and she began to tremble. Mostafa hugged her again, saying, 'It's only until tomorrow! Tonight I'm going to get some money. Right? Tomorrow morning we'll leave this place, and I'll take you to a very, very beautiful spot, prettier than heaven!'

Again there was that same patch of sky, this time suddenly bright and deep.

'There is no such place,' repeated Shahrzad.

It did exist; Mostafa believed it. Just one night stood between them and happiness; only a few hours. Life is an extraordinarily good thing, something one can love.

Mostafa put his finger under Shahrzad's chin, raising her head, but she kept her eyes on the floor. A moment later, her face seemed to brighten with a look of pure and profound understanding, and she smiled unconcernedly. She nodded uncertainly and said to herself, 'So, I've got to spend the night here; this is my home for now!'

She looked around; life here was very different, wholly unlike what she had been used to, and hardly a continuation of her old existence. Then she brought her hand to her shoulder, but, instead of touching it, let it hover in the air. The thing she wanted to remove, the something extra, the painful, bothersome thing, was not something outside of her; it was part of her being.

Mostafa left, and she looked up; night had begun, and the window was dark. 'Should I sleep?' she asked herself. She looked around and imagined that, hidden in the air, there were mysterious particles, which, if she fell asleep, would reveal their noxious nature. But, at the same time, she was certain her present state was the continuation of a dream, picking up again after a long pause.

In life's difficult moments her mother was always saying prayers for her: *The Answerer of all Needs, The Divider of Light and Salt,* and *The Healer of Old Age and Madness.* Now there was need of a great power, a recreation that would help things: the trees, stones, bodies of water. She felt a chill on her skin and fell asleep lying on her back.

Suddenly, from the depths of a pit, which, it seemed, was the source of darkness, a blinding white light flashed, then went out. In the absence of the source of light, a halo appeared, suspended in the midst of the darkness; it ignited the fine particles floating in the air like tiny flares. She thought that her life, everything that had happened to her up to that point, had emerged from the pit and, necessarily, would return to it.

The particles moved toward her, making humming sounds; she didn't hear them, but they were completely real and tangible to her. The sounds had colors. What a strange dream! Someone, evidently in terrible pain, cried out; there was a belittling roar, followed by a curse. Then she stroked her body in a purely instinctive way; this was all she possessed, and they were battling over it.

At precisely that moment, a young man on the other side of town was dreaming the same dream, and Shahrzad on her dark journey suddenly came face to face with him. At that exact moment the dream ended, but the young man was still there, in the air in the cell.

The only part of the dream worth holding onto, he was now standing in the darkness. At that precise moment they were both dreaming that they were facing each other, and suddenly she sensed that a basic part of her being, apart from her physical self, was floating in space and moving away from her at an incredible speed.

There was no choice but to wait until dawn. The young man stood there, and it seemed as though it was the very absence of light that illuminated him. Shahrzad was sure that in the past, distant or more recently, she had spent one night, or several, or, rather, her entire life in this black, cramped cell. Suddenly she asked herself, 'What became of my childhood, my dreams?'

As things stood, these were not very significant thoughts; the only important thing was the pit, the black, sucking pit.

19

Mostafa said, 'You're like a mother to everyone; but you're like a stepmother to me!'

'You don't believe me?' said Mirza. 'Just go in the basement and look under my floor cushion; whatever I have is there.'

'Forget I asked, man! Forget it!'

He waved his hand as if to say again: 'Forget it.' Then he lifted his pack from the ground. Skeptical, Khanjan said, 'Actually it's been quite a while since they sent you on a mission! Besides, since when do you have to pay out of your own pocket on a mission?'

In the hallway, Mostafa tied the pack containing his clothes to the back of his motorcycle. He lifted the kickstand, turned to his mother and said, 'Do you think it's in my hands?'

Mostafa wheeled his motorcycle into the alley. Khanjan followed him, saying, 'So what do you do with the salary you get? A person's got to save for a rainy day, no?'

More upset than ever, Mostafa said, 'It isn't like they pay me all that much!'

Then he added, 'Shit,' and spit on the floor. Khanjan asked, 'Where are you going now?'

'I told you, it's secret. I still don't know myself,' said Mostafa.

Khanjan looked up at the sky, which was overcast, quiet, and starless. She said, 'How about breakfast? At least take a bite of bread with you!'

Mostafa said nothing, got on the motorcycle, and turned the key.

Khanjan said, 'When will you be back?'

Mostafa stepped on the gas, and all Khanjan heard was: 'I don't know; I'll call you.'

She stood in the doorway until Mostafa had turned from the alley into the street. Then she closed the door and went inside. She looked out the window, wondering whether it was time to pray. Holding her hands together, she walked to the dark entrance to her room, then looked back at the doorway once more.

Mostafa circled Ferdowsi Square and exited from the northern end; bathed in a squalid, white light, the ancient poet stood, asleep on his cement pedestal. Mostafa stepped on the gas, and the motorcycle flew.

He stopped at a red light in front of the amusement park. 'Shit,' he muttered, and looked around. The spokes of the monstrous Ferris wheel shone through the tall leafless branches of the plane trees, lending the half-dark dawn sky a terrifying, supernatural look. 'Shit,' he repeated, and spit.

Night in Tehran was noiseless, but from the early morning there would be clamor and cries from all the streets, alleys, squares, homes, and shops in the city. For now it was quiet, as if it were dead.

The predawn sweepers were cleaning the streets, and the sky in the east was gradually losing its color. Cats, continually hissing, rummaged through scraps in sacks of garbage left beside the ditches lining the road.

Fed up, Mostafa shook his head. Ignoring the light, which was still red, he turned left and from the highway entered a short, broad street that veered to the right and led to a steep slope. Before the slope there was a mosque with strings of green lights hanging from its finials. At the foot of the slope, fractured rays of light shone from a bakery.

Mostafa drove down the sloping street, stopping for a moment to look at the red opening of the baker's oven. Then he stepped on the gas again, and, after crossing a narrow street with a couple of gentle hills and lined on both sides with a row of derelict huts, reached the prison building. He clearly heard the sounds of rushing water in the stream that came from the village of Darakeh, and passed the prison.

A powerful searchlight mounted on the tip of a steel post attached to the huge iron gate beamed a blinding light at him and illuminated the broad compound. Mostafa stood in the circle of light and signaled to the sleepy guard by switching his headlamp on and off. It was here he finally felt on his face the cold sting of autumn, which blew down from the peak and was laden with the dampness of snow.

A few moments later a door in the large gate opened, and Mostafa, his motorcycle still running, entered the compound. He knew the guard.

'So early in the morning, Mostafa?' the guard asked.

Mostafa wheeled his motorcycle to the wall and nodded irritably. He turned to the guard and said, 'They won't leave me in peace, Seyyed! I've got to go on a mission!'

Seyyed closed the gate and said, 'It's gotten cold!'

He rubbed his hands together and scampered back to the guardroom. Mostafa parked the motorcycle by the room. He unwound his scarf, which had been wrapped around his neck and partially covered his face, and went up the hill.

The grounds were open to the wind, which seemed to have picked up, making a howling sound. In the autumn, with the days growing shorter, there was no interval between morning prayers and the beginning of the day. This meant the sky wouldn't be entirely light when the sound of the Qur'an being recited echoed throughout the prison; every wing would suddenly come to life, and commotion would reign. Now, however, the whole place was quiet. When Mostafa reached the women's wing, he took a coin from his pocket and tapped it on the window. Soon a light went on. The guard emerged from his room, and, seeing Mostafa, took out his keys. Mostafa put his hand on the door, and, before the lock had turned fully, he pushed on it. The guard hurriedly pulled back and at the same time asked, 'What's your rush?'

Mostafa ran down the hallway straight to Shahrzad's cell. He pushed back the hatch in the door and looked inside. The cell was dark. Mostafa pounded on the door, but there was no response.

He went back to the office, where the nightwatchman, Karim, was napping behind a beat-up desk. Mostafa's tapping and the sounds of his footsteps failed to wake Karim; however, when the door opened he sat up, and, when he saw

Mostafa, he rubbed his eyes and said, 'This early in the morning? Hope everything's okay?'

Mostafa said, 'Not for me! Mr. Keramat rang, telling me to bring out the girl.'

Karim, still rubbing his eyes, asked, 'Which girl?'

'That tramp's accomplice! Shahrzad Bakhtiari!'

Now completely awake, Karim was baffled and looked at him. Mostafa went behind the desk and pulled a ring of keys from a drawer and, with Karim staring at him open-mouthed, left the room.

At the end of the hallway he put the key in the lock and opened the cell door. He stood there for a moment, and suddenly he was stricken with fear. Humans possess something which allows their presence to be felt even if it's dark, or if they can't be seen; just by virtue of being, one can feel they are around. Mostafa knew this instinctively; nevertheless, he entered the cell and, with the tip of his shoe, pushed aside the crumpled blanket lying in the middle of the room. She wasn't there; the cell was empty. He galloped back to Karim.

He planted his fists on the desk and, leaning forward, said, 'Where is she?'

Mostafa's eyes flashed with fear. After all, didn't he put her in Karim's care? Karim drew back; Mostafa hadn't closed the door behind him, and cold air from the hallway was filling the office.

Karim asked, 'Who?'

'I told you!' Mostafa said impatiently.

Yawning, Karim said, 'Oh, yeah.'

Then he nodded unconcernedly, or, perhaps feigning unconcern, asked, 'You said that Mr. Keramat called you?'

Mostafa shook the length of his whole body, appearing openly, obviously upset.

Karim smirked and said, 'Tell Mr. Keramat he's dreaming, and should go back to sleep!'

Mostafa opened his mouth to say something, but couldn't. He stared at Karim expectantly and, without knowing it, took a few steps back, as if distance was necessary for understanding what he needed to hear.

Peeking at Mostafa through half-closed eyes, Karim yawned for the second time or, maybe, pretended to do so. Whatever the case, he said, 'God have mercy on her! She was very obstinate; she said nothing, not a word, not even a syllable . . .'

Mostafa reached out and grabbed Karim's throat. Then, with his eyes shut, Karim let out a few dry coughs. Suddenly he opened his eyes and panted.

'Mr. Keramat screamed at her, "No more stories! I've had it with them!" I've never seen him so furious!'

Although he couldn't hear him properly, Mostafa nodded.

'She played dumb! Even though everything was out in the open, she didn't say a word about who gave her the weapon that she had given that tramp! Mr. Keramat had gotten all the big shots to talk, but, compared to them, she was stone silent!'

Karim rubbed his hands together and said, 'It was the middle of the night when he told them to take her up the hill and finish her off. Mr. Keramat didn't want to endure the bloody hell that her friend caused us all over the last month . . .'

Mostafa reached behind him as if searching for something to lean on, or somewhere to anchor himself. There wasn't much in the room; its modest furnishings were typical of police stations, barracks, and government offices: a few chairs with plastic seat covers, a steel cabinet, a desk covered with a black surface and a glass top. On the desk there would be a large register, grimy on the outside, dotted with finger-prints, containing the guards' weekly schedules. There would be the requisite plastic fly swatter splattered with blood and insect parts; this served as a plaything for all who sat behind that desk. There'd also be hooks nailed to the wall, with khaki overcoats hanging from them, as well as bunches of old newspapers, a smoke-blackened kettle, and a sugar bowl without a lid, like a piece of junk; that was it.

Mostafa was trembling, but this time on the inside, where it wasn't apparent to Karim. The drawer of the broken-down desk opened with a screech, and Karim took something from it. It was a piece of paper. He stretched his hand toward Mostafa and waved the paper in the air. Mostafa appeared not to see it; there was a kind of vacant, stunned look in his eyes. Then Karim said, 'Hey, man! Take it!'

As if seeing it for the first time, Mostafa took the paper from him. Karim said, 'This was the first time one of the condemned girls told me to give her will to her interrogator!'

Mostafa unfolded the paper. It quivered in his hand as if a fan in the corner of the room were blowing on it. His eyes went blank; he couldn't read the writing and looked up help-lessly. Karim was rummaging through the desk drawer again. Mostafa blinked and looked at the paper.

'Where is this place? Is this madman right? He wants to kill me? If so, why? This was supposed to take me to a place more beautiful than heaven. I didn't know that the very, very beautiful place was the grave. What had I done to him, anyway?'

Shahrzad appeared again for a moment and drifted, lighter than air, like something fleeting or a phantom, along the narrow Lorzadeh Alley. She stopped in front of her house for a moment, turned and looked at him; then suddenly she turned the key in the lock, the door opened, and she entered. *I'll pick her up*, was the sentence going through his mind, but someone seemed to say to him, 'No, if you want her for your wife and to give birth to your children, she should stay chaste.'

Karim got up, grumbling, 'I told her, write "In the Name of God" on the top, at least. But . . . I guess the poor creature had a screw loose. See what she wrote you?'

Then he said, 'Let me make some tea . . . Oh, by the way, Mr. Keramat said we should call the family to come and pick up her clothes. He said you'd have the number.'

Karim took the kettle from the wide window ledge behind him and went around the desk. Mostafa put his hand on his shoulder. Karim turned to him and said, 'Huh?'

He stood there, waiting; their faces were close. Karim asked, 'Something wrong?'

There was the sound of heavy breathing. Mostafa's eyes were on fire, his jaws were grinding.

Karim said, 'You're trembling, son!'

An old hand compared to Mostafa, Karim had seen lots of these last-minute executions. 'You'll get used to it,' he said to Mostafa.

He didn't wait for him to answer, didn't even look at him; there was no need for any discussion. He said, 'All of us get used to it, though it can be difficult at first,' and he removed Mostafa's hand from his shoulder. Then, like someone whose foot has gone to sleep, he shuffled to the door; but he stopped suddenly, shook his head, and said, 'A hot glass of tea is just the thing to set you right!' He said this with certainty mixed with a kind of deep compassion.

Mostafa was unable to stand; his knees were buckling. Walking, it seemed, would be difficult, and the chair was far away.

So Shahrzad wouldn't go to him either; death had separated her from the powerful, rich suitor. Mostafa nodded, feeling satisfied; but he suddenly found this feeling more criminal than the wrong he had just committed in his own muddled way, and it was agony to his conscience.

Karim opened the door, and cold air struck Mostafa in the face. He recoiled, stepping a few paces back, and turned to the window. Now the slightest thing seemed to make him jumpy. Karim turned to face him and wondered what had made him like this. Pondering, he failed to close the door behind him.

In the cavernous room on that quiet morning, the wing of the door stood like a toy in the hand of the malicious draught created by the cracks in the window of the room and the broken panes in the hallway. As it swung on its unoiled hinges, the screeching sound made Mostafa's hair stand on end. No, someone was actually screeching; he cupped his hands over his ears.

20

The next morning, Fattah—dressed like a groom in coat and pants, bathed in eau de cologne and with his face twice shaven—was on Lorzadeh Alley across from the Ziba Baths at house number fourteen, with a bouquet of flowers and a box of chocolates. He shifted the flowers and chocolates from one hand to the other, stopped whistling for a moment and rang the bell again.

It was a clear day, one of those fall days in Tehran, neither cold nor warm, when a person is neither happy nor sad, and being, it seems, is something fated, exactly as is not being.

What was behind the melody he whistled repeatedly? Perhaps it was a moment from that exciting afternoon when the sparrows were chirping in the bare branches of a plane tree in an old, abandoned garden. After that hurried tryst, he had been able to hear the birds singing as he lay with her in the large bedroom facing the sun, and to take in the warm, languor-inducing rays from her eyes, what eyes!

Now those eyes were in the depths of the earth, layered over with dirt.

Something else: the immense joy, which—after all those years—had granted him a perfect hardness. On that other day, when he had put his hands between her thighs as she lay on the narrow cot in his basement clinic, he had sensed the smell of death, which, inescapably, he later totally forgot, not knowing he would soon be forced to recall it.

The scent of Fattah's eau de cologne reached people kilometers away, and happiness emanated like a vapor, or something like it, from his pores. His eyes shone with an exhausting excitement and, perhaps without his being aware of it, the way he stood, stared, and moved his head—all of it—conveyed that no one was happier in the whole wide world than he was; although at the time he didn't have a clear sense of how much he and the world were alike.

He grew silent, looked at his watch, and pushed the button once more; then he began to whistle again.

Curtains folded back one by one; curious eyes, afraid or enraged, looked into the alley at the rotund, flabby man standing in front of the closed door, whistling. There was something metallic in the air, something only the people on the other side of those windows sensed; on this side were only the sun and the untroubled whistler.

What tune was it? Was it the one he was whistling, not knowing that on some future sunny day a person would separate it from the rest of the sounds in the air and realize that he, standing before the closed door, would be sending it joyfully from his lips? Would there be any sign in that detached whistle of the house with the closed door, and of the people who had inhabited it? No doubt all the folks who lived there would have died; but when it makes no difference how people lived, what difference does it make how they die?

Does the world become small, and can one recall lost memories, or trivial events? Why, whether life is bitter or sweet, does the world keep turning, the sun keep shining; why, after every spring, does summer arrive, and after every summer, autumn?

He turned and looked up and down the alley at the closed windows, the empty spaces where children, after his arrival, had suddenly stopped playing and were now behind locked doors, listening to the silence. He placed his free hand on his hip, behaving as though he were absolute master of all he surveyed: the alleys and houses, even the children behind the locked doors, who had yet to reach maturity; and even the women, who now clutched the ends of the curtains in their fists, terrified by the catastrophe that was still unknown to the man. Yes, such were the things that had been bestowed upon him, and which he humbly accepted.

He kept ringing the bell, thinking—God forbid—the electricity was out, or the bell was broken.

It never occurred to Fattah that no one was home, that his bride now lay in her grave, that Mehri, with the bundle of her daughter's clothes clasped to her stomach, was now hastily leaving Tehran on Khavaran Avenue to search for a small stretch of damp earth in some nameless cemetery. But the earth is round, and all those people who fly with great speed from one another, at some specific point will, just as rapidly, hasten back to one another. Thus must the nation go on gargling its crap, never getting its fill.

All these ideas and events belong to a world so remote one would not imagine that Fattah had ever lived in it; for him, today was still a continuation of yesterday. He didn't know that a large crack had opened between the two days, a crack that gaped like a grave.

About the Author

Amir Hassan Cheheltan was born in 1956 in Tehran, Iran, and studied electrical engineering in England, during which time he began publishing collections of short stories. To date, Cheheltan has published eight novels, five volumes of short stories and a screenplay in Tehran. His writing focuses on Iran, and the everyday issues of daily life and survival are central themes, set against the backdrop of the country's unsettled history and the interaction between religion, the state and modernization.

Due to censorship, his first novel, *The Mourning of Qassem*, was not published until 2003, twenty years after it was written, and many of his novels have had to undergo revisions before they could be published. Following harassment and threats after the publication of his work, he and his family moved to Italy for two years. His novel *Revolution Street* was first published in 2009 in German, and has yet to be published in Iran.

Cheheltan also writes essays and feature articles in the *Frankfurter Allgemeine Zeitung*, *Frankfurter Allgemeine Sonntagszeitung*, *Die Süddeutsche*, *Die Zeit*, and other newspapers. He was editor in chief of the online literature magazine *Sokhan* until 2004, a judge of the Sadegh Hedayat Literature Award for Short Stories until 2005, and a board member of the Iran Writers' Association from 2001 to 2004. He also supervises the creative writing workshop at the Karnameh Culture Centre in Tehran.

About the Translator

Paul Sprachman teaches Persian at Rutgers University. He has worked and studied in Afghanistan and Iran, and is the translator of a number of works from Persian including *Plagued by the West* by Jalan Al-e Ahmad, *A Man of Many Worlds: The Diaries and Memoirs of Dr. Ghasem Ghani*, *Journey to Heading 270 Degrees*, by Ahmad Dehqan, and *Chess with the Doomsday Machine* and *A City under Siege* by Habib Ahmadzadeh, He is also the author of *Suppressed Persian: An Anthology of Forbidden Literaure*, *Language and Culture in Persian*, and *Licensed Fool: The Damnable, Foul-mouthed 'Obeyd-e Zakani*.